Catharine Amy Dawson Scott

Idylls of Womanhood

Catharine Amy Dawson Scott

Idylls of Womanhood

ISBN/EAN: 9783337365837

Printed in Europe, USA, Canada, Australia, Japan

Cover: Foto ©Andreas Hilbeck / pixelio.de

More available books at **www.hansebooks.com**

IDYLLS OF
WOMANHOOD

BY

C. AMY DAWSON

AUTHOR OF "SAPPHO"

LONDON
WILLIAM HEINEMANN
1892

To

F. P. C.

THIS BOOK IS DEDICATED

IN

REVERENT AFFECTION

BY

THE AUTHOR

CONTENTS

A WOMAN'S ETHICS

OUT of the deeps of the valley, the shadowy deeps grey-
 green,
Where the glimmer of twilight water, steals up thro'
 ascending glooms,
And the pines are a whispering darkness, clear-sketched
 in the after-glow
Of a sun-god slain in his berserk, and slain with his face
 to the foe,—
Out of the deeps we toiled, and found the leaves on the
 lawn
Tossed in a windy swirl, a dance of russet and brown,
Tossed and scattered and torn, as thou and I in the
 past,
The past that is folded in dark, as our dead in the silence
 of God.

And I felt with the wind on my brow, and the stretch of
 the golden skies
A-deepening down the hills, till their radiance gathered
 and passed

And only the eyelid of wisdom, might hold the sun-beauty
foreseen

And evolved thro' the numberless ages of mist, and
chaos, and dark—

I felt that the pain must have speech, that the life of my
innermost life,

The life that was hushed in despair, as a spring in the
caves of the sea,

Must rise, heart-ruddied and rise, till it broke thro' the
billows of sleep,

Till it ran up the weed wet beaches, and shallowed away
and was lost,

A scattering echo of grief, that is stilled by the dirge of
the deep.

Friend—friend of my noon—of the dawning and strife of
my day

My friend to hearken and heed, tho' the lapsing cloud-
heavy years

Have burdened thee sore with a sorrow, an infinite
sorrow—God wots—

Not grief like my absolute grief, a pool that is stagnant
and still ;

Not death like that absolute death, that is held in the
dying of love,

But parting—the parting of souls—the parting of souls
for an hour,

Or less—for the space of a cry, of a wind-echoed wandering wail.

Not you to forget how we dreamed, when the larch new-
tasselled with green

Swayed over our heads in the woodland, and brown on
the bloom-white spray

Swelled the throats of the songsters warbling of summer-
rich glooms and gold.

We dreamed, and our dream was a hero- a Galahad
virgin-pure

With a face like the freshness of morning and thoughts
unsoiled as the light,

When it leaps thro' the heavens aflush, gold-spearing the
recreant shades.

And we vowed standing deep in the mosses, we vowed by
the bonds of our love,

By our sisters lost in the cities, by womanhood's weakness
and strength,

That the men we would wed should be pure, should be
pure of all sensual sin

As the Christ and our maiden souls, we vowed it and
turned again,

Threading the tangle of grasses, and wandering deep in
the wood.

We dreamed when the rose was in bud, and before the
full flush of the flower

Had lighted the gardens, and given its golden-sweet heart
to the sun,

One came from the city—your hero, a scholarly man and
grave,

Wise with the wisdom of science, a thinker, a worker and more—

Yet who knew not of love, was content to search out beginnings of truth ;

A man half-asleep—but you spoke, and he roused as the warrior afar,

Who hears the faint note of the clarion, the echo of thundering feet,

All the turmoil and hurry of conflict, and stumbles full-armed to his feet ;

A man with the faults of his manhood, but filled with an earnest desire

To learn, as a child of its mother, to climb, groping upwards and on,

Till he paused on the levels of love, the levels where God meets the soul

And sanctifies, purifies, burns, till the dross has been parted, and leaves

The pure metal, the gold, the love-gold, the element matchless and rare,

So rare in our pitiful world, that we blend it and tinker and spread,

Just its gleam on the poor wooden frame of the daub that we show as a life.

Thus were dreams over-filled ere the summer had deepened the green of the beech ;

You wedded, and from the white roadway the thunder of galloping hoofs

Smote chill on my heart—tho' the lilies yet lifted their
    pride by the way,
And the lark was triumphantly trilling his story of music
    and love.
You left me, a girl in the flower and flush of impetuous
    youth,
A girl with a scattering of gold where now is the greyness
    of time.
And behold, now the autumns are ten, since we trod the
    brown leaves under foot,
(Half-a-score of hot years! so o'erfilled with labour and
    earnest desire
To lift the dark earth out of pain and the seethings and
    urgings of sin,
That our hands have not touched) you return, but alas in
    the shadow of loss,
You return, but your footsteps are lonely, you stretch out
    a tremulous hand
For help—and remember. Oh death, of the mystic "one
    flesh" making twain,
Making twain with a rattle of bones with skeleton faces
    a-grin,
Methinks thou wert wanton in snatching, when others
    had leapt at thy call,
Merry footing to tunes of despair, to the echo of clods
    on a grave.

And I? Well he came in the autumn, a man happy-
    hearted and hot,

With laughter laid under his lashes, a man of intangible
    charm,
But you know it—the charm of one man for one woman,
    the charm
That is love at first sight, the dim knowledge that here is
    our nature's completion ;
He came, but my meadows were many, my gold as the
    wheat of a land,
And he was but a soldier, the son of a race that had
    sprung from the soil
In the near yesterday.   So they spake, and my lover went
    forth in his pride,
In a madness of pain, that must burn, tho' he steeped it
    in passion and sin.

The days grew apace into months, but the dew of the
    morn was a tear,
A pathos now lurked in the valley, a sorrow lay dark on
    the hill,
And the woodland was ever a whisper that throbbed with
    the sadness of love,
While all music was mystery, yearning—a tremor of
    memories awake—
The murmurous sound of a voice, a voice that was sweet
    in my ear
As the nightingale's song.   Standing rich in their bind-
    ings of vellum and calf,
Were the tomes that my fathers had gathered, the
    thoughts of the wonderful dead,

And I learnt, sitting low at their feet, until life seemed a
    moment of time,
And my pain but the breath of a weed that has rooted
    and bloomed among flowers—
Till rich with the wisdom of ages, and walking in meadows
    of thought,
I learnt an endurance of all things. Elaine had been
    many-year wife
To his brother, and widowed now dwelt, within neigh-
    bourly distance—a friend,
With a tongue that must ever be pouring its runnel of
    wearisome chat,
Yet *his* sister and therefore—a friend. One languorous
    storm-heavy gloam,
When mists lay dense on the marsh and the waves of a
    whitening sea
Heaved greyly and fell, we were sitting in dusk of a
    darkening room,
And dropping her voice to a whisper, she spake of men's
    folly, the sin
Of one man among others—my love. I turned with the
    thrust in my heart,
Turned dumbly and left her—the fires of a shrinking and
    sensitive shame
Ablaze in my soul, ruddy flames, that flickered and
    brightened and burnt,
Till the sweetness of love, its white honour, its purity,
    patience and trust,
Were as weeds on a smouldering heap—or the ash of a
    funeral pyre.

But out in the gloom of the woods where branches were
   wailing the storm,
For the winds with a wakening sough had crept out of
   their caves and away,
And the sea had a moan in its murmur, a prescient
   sorrowful moan—
I could suffer. The plash of the rain and the quiver of
   loose-leaping light
Were round and above me, with crash of the mutinous
   thunder, but deep
In my world-hidden glen, was a strife more deadly, for
   faith had been bruised,
And the patience that comes from unfaith is a patience
   akin to despair.

The storm-pinions folded again and the day that had
   wounded my life,
Beyond healing and hope laid its head on the merciful
   bosom of night,
But the dawns that should be, must follow and creep from
   the arms of the east,
Must redden the apples and change, must scatter the
   yellowing leaves,
Till the first hoar-frost of the winter stole over the
   meadows, and took
The old life from its chair by the ingle. I rose up as
   carelessly free
As the wind in the pines—and behold, as a face at the
   window—*my love.*

Oh God! but his kiss of betrothal yet burned on my
tremulous lips,
And the ring of his voice was as sweet, as when erst he
had murmured of love.
Was it mine to deny him and pause, to stifle the hunger
that leapt
To answer caress with caress and to cry in the term of
our vow :
"The man whom I wed must be pure, must be pure of
all sensual sin
As the Christ and my maiden soul?"   I spake it, and
whitened again
As the answer grew on his cheek, with never denial or
word.

When the dizzy beatings of pain had lessened their
clamorous throbs,
I pleaded : "Oh wrong of all wrongs, to betray with a
promise of love,
Wrong to her, to the world, and to me, a smirch of dishonour and shame
On the arms that you bear.   For the sake of the woman
who cradled thy youth,
Who pointing to purity ever, would show thee the way ;
for the sake
Of one who would hold to thine honour as men overboard
to a rope—
Turn back to this flower of the meadows, this flower thou
hast crushed in the way.

Before God thou hast made her thy wife, and God shall
 require it of thee.
Dost thou think, that because man has muttered no
 sanctified form of bald words
Over thy union, it was the less marriage, with God for
 the priest of thy vows ? "

He answered with specious assertion, men were not as
 maids, and his love
Had been mine without swerving or change. For his
 sin ? it had been but a slip,
A passing temptation, an impulse. " Alas, when the sum
 of our deeds
Is told over in infinite time, and we render our sorry
 account,
The terrible searchings of truth shall be turned on each
 paltry excuse,
Till it shrivel and blacken and fall as a moth that is
 caught by the flame.
Before God—men and women are bound to be equally
 honest, as pure
The man as the woman—'fore God ! Men have tinkered
 humanity's laws,
Till the woman so dwells in injustice, her faith is merged
 into a doubt
Of all justice eternal or earthly. Oh heart by the love
 that is crown
Of our sorrow, turn back to thy choice, turn back as a
 bird to its mate.

Oh love tho' our hearts must be torn, until life seem a
    vision of pain,
Give me back what is dearer than love, my faith in the
    man I have set
After God in my worship, the faith that you only can give
    me again."

Sore was the strife, but he yielded—I knew not the thing
    that I asked,
Yet if this were the wage of his sin—ay me, but his very
    consent
Given slowly and grudged was an anguish, an anguish
    edged doubly and sharp
As a knife 'twixt the shoulders, a word, that smote on my
    heart as it fell.
The country was silent in snow as we whirled thro' the
    desolate land,
And saw in a sparkle of sunlight, the spires of the city
    arise
With the prayerful breath of the few. We questioned in
    alley and court,
Till we found her, a girl very pretty, but flighty and
    garish and loud,
A little dim soul that had walked in the dark amid
    pitfalls and slipped.

And in dusk of a rain-heavy dawning, they stood by the
    altar, a gloom
Of dim aisles stretching westward in stillness, a hush on
    the belfry above.

But I turned from the mutter of voices, the murmurs of
  wedding assent,
The promise of love that had faded, of honour that was
  but a name,
To look through the brightening window, where laughter
  of riotous light
Had lifted the curtains of cloud ; and I prayed, "Oh
  Father, Thy strength !
For the burden is heavy to bear, the thorns without ever
  a rose,
And I very human and weak, oh weak as a soft-footed
  babe
That would hold to its mother and venture."   I prayed,
  and was answered in strength,
Not mine, nor of me, but a gift ; and could gather the girl
  in my arms,
Mine to hold, mine in patience, in love—a bride whom
  her husband disdained,
Who nor answered his rough-laid commands, his careless
  farewell, nor his touch,
An indifferent kiss, a hand-clasp, but looked outward, her
  glance on the grime
Of the London-dark houses.   Yet thick in forget-me-not
  eyes stood the tears,
As his ship, moving out of her moorings, unfurled her
  swan-wings, and the mist
Enfolded her swift in its silver, its moon-silver veilings of
  light.

The glamour of winter yet rested on meadow and forest
    and hill,
With a silence of slumber that stiffened the shadows adown
    in the dells,
And deepened the rest of the woodland, stretching the
    icicle down
From the thatch-covered eaves of the cottage, and leaving
    a wonder of leaves
In frost on the casement ; and we, two souls that were
    nearing in love
Went to sick and to sad in the village, the crisping rime
    on the ruts
Of the winding desolate street, I, teaching, a word and a
    thought,
And she, as a field in the spring, that is softened by sorrow
    in snow,
A field that is fit for the plough, and the after sowing of
    seed.
For deep in her heart was a spark, neither coldness nor
    absence might quench,
And the flash of her love made as daylight our dusk of
    monotonous years.

Oh ! hey for the roses of summer, the sun-mellowed sweet-
    ness of June !
When the bushes awake into crimson, the richness of
    verdure and bloom,
And a pale moss-bud is the chosen, the queen of the
    blossoming boughs,

That nod out their honey-fragrance, in languorous scents
    of the noon.

She gathered the wealth of the roses, and turning had
    broken the stem

Of a single moon-silver lily, a pure thing widened at
    dawn

From bud into perfect bloom, and was standing, the
    flush of her youth

Clear-shining in eyes of affection, as sun-brightened waters
    at dawn—

A wife all as fair as the roses, as pure as the lily she
    held,

And as sweet as the fragrance of summer—a wife all as
    lovely as Eve

In the Biblical legend—sweet Eve, ere Adam had roused
    from his sleep.

And a stranger who leant on the gate, hushed, marvelled
    a little, and came

Crying, in love-happy accents, the accents and words that
    were mine,

" Wife ! is it you? My wife ! Oh, why was this womanly
    grace

Undreamed of my heart, all the years that I wandered
    away and away ! "

And I, who had sat at the window, day-dreaming a little,
    and sad,

Caught my breath in a sob.   It was well.   For this I had
    laboured and prayed ;

For this I had given my hope of a love that should answer
    my own ;

For this—oh, All-Father forgive ! but the passionate pain
    is alive

As an arrow-head deep in the flesh.   It is well ; but the
    anguish— Oh, God !

Is there salve for me none ?   Be content, little heart, that
    has gained its desire.

He loves her, and thou art forgotten ; thy patience has
    earned its reward.

True husband, he loves without stain.   When the harvest
    is cut from the earth,

Who cares that it grew on a grave and browned over sleep
    of the dead ?

The Past is a book which is closed till an Infinite Love
    shall unfold

And blot out its errors.   We seek after happiness rather
    than good ;

And yet in our innermost souls we know it were better to
    leave

The feast and the frolic of youth, the soberer sweetness of
    age

To pace through the desert alone, and forgotten as love
    can forget—

Than to sit down content with dishonour, to sit down
    content.   Oh, sweet eyes !

That are dim with the sorrow of others, love smites with
    so heavy a hand,

And we are so weak, not a leaf, tossed high in the sport
of the wind,
Not a dew-flashing spearlet of grass, but is stronger to
bear and abide.

Lo ! Diana has deepened her silver, and shines as a
crescent of gold,
A light on the hill and a shadow, a darkness in deeps of
the vale ;
The moan of the wandering wind has eddied away, and
the panes
Of the low-browed cottages gleam, each pane with a tiny
ray,
The light of a labouring household—father and wife and
babe.
But the earnest touch of your fingers, oh, Mary ! is calling
me back,
And a murmur of patience arises ; of patience content with
its day,
A patience that taketh no thought, and asketh no hope,
but is glad
In its duties, as once long ago, before sorrow and love
were acquaint.

NURSE, is he coming? set the door ajar
That I may hear the thud of horse's hoofs
That side the river, hear it above all
The deafening beats of blood that whisper " death !"
To die ! to fold my hands in prayer, and leave
What shall be to the father-mother care
Of the All-loving, this hot agony
Or hellish pain, sleep-withered as a leaf
Which the night frosts have nipped, and all my griefs
Turned to the numbness of yon marble urn !
Dead ! my griefs dead ? This heart-ache as a pang
That is forgotten, and my yearnings hushed
As though they had not been ? If death could bring
A sure forgetfulness he were not held
So terrible, as sweet. And yet to leave
The cycling of my love—a faithless moon,
Deserting its wan planet for an age
Of solitary whirling through the heavens ;
To leave friends—kindred—home—nay then such loss
Were less than nought in this dark hour of pain,
When I must leave—not home, nor kin, nor friends,
But only Mark, my Mark——

B

                              A step that rings
On the resounding flags ! it comes—alas,
The echoes answer faintly, and it dies
Upon the hill, as yet another hour
Is counted from the steeple.   Though he spur
The gallant roan, I may not hope to hear
The sudden splash of riders at the ford,
Until the freshness of the dawn has dewed
The sweet lush grass, and every yellow eye
That opens on the mead.   The night is chill,
Or I am numb with cold of creeping death;
So numb, the pain has gathered round my heart,
And life is but a yearning, an intense
Strong prayer, too deep for issue of poor words—
That I may linger till these tired eyes
Have looked again on that stern-featured face,
Which in the long ago I learnt to love—
Oh not too well, when once we break the box
It needs must follow that the precious oil
Will spill its golden fragrance drop by drop
Upon the chosen life.   Come hither, Nurse,
Your watching will not bring him, and I fear
To pass with all this weight of craving love,
These tarnished memories and the secret hurt
That sapped my joy, unspoken.   In that hush
Whose gloom is even now about my feet,
The hidden burden of my life might press
Too heavily upon my sleeping soul
For quiet rest, and I be roused to walk
As other wandering souls about the world,

Until the trump of doom. So sit you nigh
Till I can find the outlet of sad words,
And with their bitter, hasty overflow
Loosen the ice the ice about my soul.

Mark was my father's godson, and the child
Of an old comrade who had left his dull
And wifeless age, this tender legacy.
My father's godson and his heir; a strong
And merry presence in the ancient halls
That gloomed above a student and his books.
But ere my Mark had sown his college oats,
The old man's fancy chanced upon a maid
Who took the picture for its golden frame,
The shrunken thinker for his lands and wealth—
And I was born, as Isaac, a weak thing,
Which yet was destined to stretch out a hand,
And snatch at Ishmael's promised heritage.
I wronged my Mark in living, and the toss
And tangle of this after time have grown
From those unnecessary breaths, which laid
My hapless mother in her grave.

        I lived,
But did not think to play as other babes,
Being uncertain of my strength, and sad ;
With memories of a near eternity,
Yet looking from my wistful eyes, and death
Beckoning ever with my mother's hand.
Yet did I struggle out of infancy
As lilies grow, a slender stem, a leaf,

Grass-like and poor, and a yet hidden flower ;
And all my joy was in the whispering woods,
Where the brown rabbit brushed th' uncurling brake,
While under tassels of the larch, the pale
Blue mist of bells chimed out a honey-breath,
And overhead in solemn gathering
The rooks debated, and a wanderer sailed
Into the red heart of the setting sun.
To sit and watch, sometimes to read—till all
The mighty volumes ranged along the shelves
Of that dim room wherein my father wrote,
Were as wise friends, not wholly understood
But studied—was the solace of a youth,
So lonely that the very thrushes sang
Beside it unaffrighted.   The old man
Bowed under the hoar burden of his years,
Till Time had counted eighty and yet eight.
And then he, dying, called my Mark again
From where he laboured in a foreign town ;
Saying, " If I was father to thy youth
Prove it this day, and take the child I leave
Into thy ward.   Take her—her lands—her gold
And make them thine—so shall I die content,"
And flushing with some memory of youth,
He turned the pathos of dim eyes, that strove
And strove in vain to pierce the mists of death—
On Mark.   " You do not love ? " he said, and stayed
Until the face before him with a flash
Of love and pride and easy confidence,
Dispelled the doubt ; " Love is a thing apart,

For idlesse or for earnest, and my life
Has been too full of labour, for much stir
Or heat of passion—therefore am I free ;
And Mildred from this hour shall be my ward—
My charge—my wife, that so I may repay
In slender measure all the store of love
Expended on my drifting orphan-hood."

So were we wedded ere my father died,
A scholar and a wilding of the woods !
But each as other ignorant of love,
And the deep mystery of dual life—
Not passion but the breaking down of walls
That stretch between us and the sympathy
Of kindred natures—the free intercourse
Of souls that loving once, shall never more
Be closed in loneliness.   We pledged the dim
Unknown of days, sowing the seed of ill
With prayers, and vowing an enduring love
That could not be, as lightly as a child
Might swear to compass deeds of Heracles;
For neither knew the sin of wedding-bonds
That bind no love, and in white ignorance
Must choose the downward path.
                              Too weak to bear
The myriad petty cares of household rule,
And over young for wifehood, I was sent
To a dull London school, where leaves and buds
And laughter of the dryads of the woods,
Were as the memory of light, to some

Blind captive ; there in pale routine, to shut
The date of battles in a brain, that searched
All history for the might of hero-thoughts,
And loathed to hear of wanton strife, of hosts
Slain by some ruffian warrior, and the rude
Blood-staining of the innocent green sward.
For two long tedious years I strove to learn
All fair refinements that a county dame—
To whom the still-room is more beautiful
Than any glade bemossed and flower-strewn,
With wide boughs nearing the green earth, and glad
Brown waters brawling on their lilied way—
Should know.   But ere I parted from my nook,
The bent arm of an oak, to walk sedate
Through lordly London streets, my husband spake
Of all that I must grow before he came
To claim me as his bride, and though so young,
I lifted my white eyelids to his height,
And found him not too lordly, for the close
Barred chamber of my heart to have and hold,
So loved him with the fervour of a youth
That had gone lonely since its cradle-days.

As the too slender lily spreads its bud
Into a star, and breaks upon the world,
I wakened from my pallid maidenhood,
To see a regal loveliness, of fair
Sun-glorious hair, as a rich halo shine
About my brows ; and trembling as they spake
Of eyes that might have lighted a wan saint

A Woman's Love

In mediaeval times to angel-hood,
I dared not taste the pleasure of this strange
New loveliness, until my husband's praise
Should crown it as desirable and sweet.
Alas! for the still visions of the night,
And all the light ambitions that are hid
Behind the front of ignorance! When Mark
Kissed me farewell beneath those spinster-eyes,
That held the touch of even wedded lips
Well-nigh a sin, his brow was clear as mine,
A virgin-brow that knew no grief nor lack,
But bent its gravity upon the world
In calm and studious coldness. Yet when time
Had closed my pupilage and he returned
To claim his bride, the glooms of some regret
Were darkling 'neath his lids. I saw their gleam,
And shivered as a man upon whose grave
Some stranger walks, noting the chilly glance
That dwelt upon my beauty but was moved
No whit, and the half wistful tenderness,
Which to a wiser heart had said: "We two
Are bound in law, and have a friendly love
Each for the other, we must be content
To live the long years in a kind accord
Which knows no passion."

                              As upon my lips
Reserve had laid its silences, I raised
No questioning, but laid my hand in Mark's,
With gladness of a trusting child, which takes

An offered kindness as the test of love.
A horse's gallop, or the wind? oh nurse,
I think, mine ears would waken to his tread
Tho' clay lay heavy on my breast, and dank
Dull autumns have left twenty seasons' leaves
Upon the mould that wrapped my winding-sheet.
Only the wind? the wind among the elms?
A whisper sad as breaking waves that beat
Thro' the grey ages with incessant moan
On some dim northern waste of rock and wrack.

He took me home—and on the levels broad,
And ever broader stretched the swathes of light ;
Till roses, flushing, changed the gold to red
And climbed the ancient gables, shedding sweet
Blush-petals over all the velvet lawns.
And there, in harmony of life, we stayed
Till five long years had crowned our wedding-vows
And changed into a memory, so sweet
That tho' I die to-night, without that love
Which was my prayer, I yet am half content
Having that five-year memory of peace.
My husband was a father to my youth
Most tender—teaching—training, till my thought
Could move with his thro' all the world of books.
So tender that I ripened as a peach
Upon the south side of a sheltering wall,
For having never known the signs of love,
Nor seen its fire as summer-lightning leap
From a man's eyes, I knew no want nor flaw

In Mark's regard, but was content, as those
In cavern-pools who take their dusky light,
To be as the sun-radiance of a world.

We went one August when the bines were bent
(From where they over-ran the tallest poles
And should have fluttered in the breezy air—,
By golden weight of hops, across the fields
To meet some county notables and dine
With a new-wedded cousin of my Mark's.
And as I sat conversing of this maid,
And that fair infant, how to bake and brew,
And what good bargains Lady Ann had bought
At the forced sale, a-weary yet constrained
To aid the trifling chat, a girl was led
Towards me by my hostess.   " Norah Grant,
A cousin of your husband's and his friend
While you were yet at lessons," and I saw
A slender girl, not beautiful but strong,
A girl who had no barriers of reserve
To overleap, when any tender thought
Stirred in her soul, but turned it from her tongue,
As Nature turns a seedling which may grow
Or fall into the maw of hungry swine.
" My husband's cousin and his friend?" I saw
His eyes turn suddenly on her, and fire
With a wild joy that faded out in gloom.
And all that night I pondered on his glance,
Turning and turning till the welcome dawn
A rush of light, a flight of golden wings

Had wakened all the songsters of the wood.
" Your cousin-friend," I said, "has charmed my ear
With the sweet ripple of her speech, and I
Would ask her here.   Our dual solitude
Were nobler for some sacrifice——"

                        But Mark
Demurred a little, as he gave my brow
The morning kiss.   "Leave well alone ; the girl
Is kindly-natured, once she was my friend,
But now—oh, I am older, let her be."

Yet still we met—by chance, until our lips
Touched in the kiss of a chill cousin-hood ;
For my reserve and a close fear that lay
Beneath the sunny surface of her speech,
Forbade the nearing of our souls in love ;
Yet much we spake, as those who think and think
Thro' silence of long years, and meet at length
A comrade, who has touched the self-same hopes ;
While Mark, who held his passions as his horse
Under control, and spake no hasty word,
Nor many words at all, dwelt on her face
As I on his, until a doubt, a fear,
A dim suspicion, bitter as the drops
Of a slow poison, stirred in every hour.

I found a mystery—or fancied one
In every fervid word that moved her lips.
And she was one of those, whose greater thought
Can realise that the penurious lives

About us, are the children of one love
The sons and daughters of the Lord—not foul
Nor base nor squalid, but dim souls and sad :
Born to the sceptre of humanity,
But early bound apprentice to that wheel
Which knows no pause, until the toil-worn frame
Is laid where neither oaths, nor screams, nor blows.
Can break its quiet rest.   My own chill blood
That knew no passion of philanthropy,
Warmed in me as she spake, but still I put
The fervour by, not curious, but moved—
(By secret dread of what my hand might touch
To search, until at length one whispered it,
Not out of malice, but pure carelessness—
Or so I think—I who had been more blessed
In dying then, a happy wife, a girl
Whose hand had never chanced upon the pricks
That roses hide, than if some four-score years
Should strike their hours upon my burdened soul.

My Mark and she had met in sunnier climes,
While I was yet contenting me with husks
Of knowledge, learning ever of the bald
And evil lives of kings, of history
Which was too lofty to record the ways
And wills of the unnumbered multitudes—
Yet called itself the history of our land.
I was a child at school, enduring all
Of copies, dates and needlework that pass
For mental training with a class of maids,

When Mark beneath the chestnuts raised his eyes
To that wan face, and found it beautiful.

" Of course, my dear, his bride reclaimed his heart,
It was a passing fancy, nothing more."
And I could dully echo " Nothing more,"
Altho' a vision of the south was warm
Upon my canvas—a wide stretch of hills
Beneath the vaulting azure, and the deep
Sweet music of a babbling water-flow,
Where straying feet had brought a twain who loved,
Yet knew it not, who spake of books and song,
Perchance had read the poets of the land,
And drawn their rhythmic fervour into life.
My Mark had loved her.   Had ? I knew too well
That love with such as Mark is long as time,
And patient, oh, as patient as the sea
That creeps, and creeps, until the strand is hid.
To look and love—alas to wake and find
Its longing as a weary, weary ache
Within the breast.   Oh husband mine, that I,
Thy child-wife, should have brought so dark a doom
Upon thy life.   To long ? alas, my Mark
Thy love was answered, mine must knock and knock
At that heart-door I have no key to fit,
Must knock and be denied.   My love, my Mark—
Alas not mine—*my husband*, that at least ;
A perfect husband, bearing with my youth
In such unruffled tenderness, I deemed
Thee calm with the content of middle age,

And loving, but with manhood's reticence.
A step, dear Nurse, unbar the outer door
And let him in.   Not Mark, she tarries long—
And the night darkens with the chill of dawn.
I have not found the day so full of light.
That I can yield to the enshrouding dark
Without one sunset gleam, without one touch
Of clinging and regretful lips.   My Mark,
Had parted from his manhood's love, content
To suffer, so he kept that reckless oath
Made to a dying man.   And when the truth
Was spread before me as an open book,
Methought the bitterness and dark of death
Had closed about my life ; but when its pangs
Were somewhat dulled, and the first flush of pain,
Of passionate unreasonable pain—
As but a selfishness had been repressed—
Denied—I wakened to a softer will,
In which the self that mars our nobler deeds
Had neither place nor part.   I willed to stand
As strong before the judgment of my soul,
As they who parted under chestnut boughs
In Italy.   I loved him, Nurse, so well
That I would free him even from my love !
And yet in vain, for death has ever fled
My wooing touch.   The fever came and went,
The lightning blasted one I almost touched,
And the mad horses dashed adown the hill,
Leaving me by the way-side, but unhurt—
Alas, unhurt.   The scourge of cholera

Lashed the fen villages with death and dread,
And I was keen to succour. but must stay—
Mark's will not mine—within the boundaries
That shut our wealth from the poor lives about
Must stay secure, while he went to and fro
Untiringly among the stricken foiks.
One languid noon, when all the air was rife
With darkening pestilence, I sat to brush
Slowly and lazily, the lengthy gold
Of my loose hair, until the whining voice
Of a chance beggar stirred my reverie.
The maids had found him food, and in return
He poured the gathered gossip of the way
Into their thirsty ears. " My lady's nurse
Was stricken yesternight, and her poor babes
Are crying in the road way." Thro' the panes
Of the wide window fell a tinted light,
And as I over-leant the ancient yard
I caught the further details : " Motherless !
Oh, ay, before the night."

                The hour was mine !
For Mark was watching by a stricken man,
And would not come again before the night.
Rising, I wound the gold about my head,
And slipped away to find the stable yard
Deserted of its guardians, who were met
To drink and gossip with the maids. I led
The old white mare out of her littered stall,
And rode away, down leafy glades and o'er
The springy turf, where palest heather bloomed,

And the bees murmured round the fragrant gorse :
But when I clattered thro' the village street
It was to find the story false, that ill
On which I waited, gloomed in many a hut,
But had avoided yours, as tho' the blood
Of Paschal lambs was on the lintel-piece.
Yet even in that hour my prayers were heard !
The mare was old, and as we turned, she caught
Her hoof among the cobble-stones and fell.
I knew an agony of pain, an hour
Of anguish crushed into a second's beat ;
And then a sudden darkness as of death
Enwrapt my sense.   Yet have I looked again
On things familiar, tho' it only stayed
My passing for a little bitter space.

My features are unharmed ?   My face as fair
As when I left the world of school a bride
So glad, so careless, and oh God, so young ?
My poor, fair face, well I am strangely glad
His eyes should gather a fair memory,
To store in the chill chambers of regret.
I die, that he may quaff the cup of joy
And yet—and yet—oh Nurse I cannot bear
To dream that other in my place, his *wife*,
A wife so well-beloved—that our six years
Of wedded happiness, will only seem
As a grey dusk that has preceded day.
I cannot bear that all my household gods,
The poor things that I touched with reverence

Of love and memory should pass to her ;
That her sweet tones grown deeper with content
And wifely joy should echo in my halls
When I am silent, that her feet should turn
To the long window that commands the road,
That she may watch, as I, for his return.
My rival and his love !   I was his wife,
Never his love, and tho' my day has stretched
Thro' lives of pain, I am so young—too young
To give up all, to lie back in the earth,
And know another woman in my place,
Yet—for his sake—
                    Oh God, let me sleep well—
Let me be hushed upon the mother-breast
Of Nature, and forget the love I missed,
The love that she will gather on the morn.
Let no dim consciousness of earth disturb
My rest, and shew their love, but deepen sleep
Till I am deaf, undreaming, dead.   For I
Not only lose this present, but the hope
Of future meeting in that after time
When life for all is as a garnered sheaf ;
For tho' love sleeps, it sleeps to rise again
And flood the halls of heaven with its light.
Must I go hungry even there ? and find
A crown of thorns within the circlet's gold ?
Nay, God is merciful, and I shall lie
Hidden in the deep hollow of His hand,
Until forgetfulness as a white worm
Has eaten all my heart.   But Nurse no word

To mar their future, let me lift the cup
Of happiness to my Mark's lips unspoiled
By any bitter drops that I may shed.
Hark there--he comes !—— The breaking of the night
Has brought the clatter, clatter of hot hoofs
Upon the rounded stones——

My Mark, my love :
There is no present need for such a fear
As damps your forehead, for I linger yet,
And for a little while.   The burning pain
Has left me numb and tired, but not too dull
To feel your presence, as a misty world
That reaches out towards the hidden sun.
The mare was old, but I forgot her years
And rode her far, what wonder that she fell ?
Alas, it was to leave me low, sweet-heart,
So low I shall not rise again to walk
Thro' household ways with you.   My fault : and I
Must suffer—nay, the suffering is done ;
I am so tired, our very parting seems
As a good night upon the edge of sleep,—
A calm good night altho' our wedded years
Have been so whitely perfect, that I would
They could be stretched and stretched till sixty years
Ay until six times sixty, till all time
Had leisurely been told.   Oh love, your care
Has made my winding way so sunny wide,
At once so sheltered, and so broad of view
O'er all the level country at our feet,
That I must falter as I bless you, I

C

Who was so young a wife, dear-heart, I wist
Not all my duty, tho' there was no hour
Wherein I did not seek to bind and loose
As you had wished.   If, in my ignorance,
I e'er had wronged you as a child might sin
Against an elder's peace, forgive it now.
At least I loved you, and the faults of youth
Are such as time may mend and patience pass.
Tears?   Oh my Mark, I am not worthy grief
So passionate, and yet it reconciles
My heart to the long sleep.   To close mine eyes
And know your tears are falling on my grave,
As showers on a green memory, is to sleep
Contented as a child in mother-arms ;
To sleep and smile, as one that in his dreams
Beholds the vision of undying love.

The cold is creeping on towards my heart,
And I have that to say before we part
Which must not be delayed—a last request—
Which like a seed must slumber in your soul
Thro' all the coming winter.

                              When the fires
Of Yule are lighted on your hearth and time
Would bring old hopes, old faces as a mist
Between you and their glow—redeem my wish ;
So shall I rest more calmly in my bed—
Two yards of earth beneath the dripping yews.
I must go hence, and yet I cannot leave

Your life to a long loneliness, content
That a pale memory should fill my place,
Smiling its misty thoughts across the board,
And keeping silence in our childless halls.
I cannot die, a frightened star that falls
And falls, until the bosom of the night
Has hushed it into sleep, with the reproach
Of all your solitary days and nights
Upon my soul.

    It is my dying wish
You bring another to your home, a heart
To mark your goings, long for your return,
And fill the nest with babble of young birds.
A maid to whom my duties will be joys—
(Hush there—the word is bitter—ay) *a wife*.
My death-dreams will be cleansed of earthly taint,
If I can know one nobler in my place,
Can trust my duties, and the household gods
I treasured, to some woman worthier
Of your regard—Love, I can scarcely see
Your dark strong face—the dawn is surely stayed,
Or is this death? One kiss, and now your hand
Warm on my clay-cold fingers—darkness—death.
But tho' I am so tired, oh Mark, to leave
You—you for ever—therein lies the sting,
And bitterness of death.

      Oh Mark, my love
The darkness shadows all—I cannot hear

Your voice, save as a far off murmuring sound,
Borne to me on the waters of this stream
That surges, surges, drifting out my soul
Towards the misty broads, a wreck, a raft,
A white sail shining in the light, and lost
Within the thickening haze.

                      Sleep? Ay, to leave
Not life, but love ; to sink beneath these waves
And never know the freshening of the deep,
To never seize the substance of our hopes—

Mark—love—to leave you—you ——

RUKHMABAI

Pahili beti Dhanachi peti *

WE sat together where the London roll
Of traffic as a dull continuous roar
Beat on the lofty windows, she and I,
An Indian with hushed memories of wrong
Beneath her patient eyelids, and a maid
Whose Irish blood must send her hotly forth
To strive with evil customs of the world,
Until the shadow-angel spreads his wing
Of darkness over the broad face of heaven.
And walled about from that incessant sea
Of faces, that has made our London sad,
We let the hours float out in changeful talk
Of Sutras, Sanhita, the ancient law
Of Manu, and that newer Brahmo-cult,†
Which asks no mediator, but would go
To the All-Father as a child who loves

* A daughter first-born is a casket of wealth.—*Hindoo proverb.*
† The Brahmo-Samaj, or church of the reformed Brahmins.

Too greatly to be fearful ; of the castes
Brahmin and Kshatrya ; of leadership
And many a usage, dim and rich and strange ;
Of eastern thought, and that wide wondrous world
Of Hindustan, the land of bodhi-trees,
Of the too-fragrant champacs, of hid pearls,
And spice, and gems, whose sand is molten gold ;
Its dusky folk in number as the drops
That falling, falling through the centuries
Have filled the mighty hollows of the earth.
A land of dreams, of old philosophies
That looked upon the morning of the world
Of dreams, alas ! that have gone out in night.
And as we talked, the drifting wave of words
Chanced in its ebb upon a darker theme—
The widowhood of little idle babes
At play with life, their wedlock ere the sweet
Bewildered eyes have visioned thro' the gates,
Which lock the heritage of deepened life
From every callow wonderer, a world
Beautiful—rich—the gems of every age
Set closely—deeply—in its prismal front.
And a quick sadness hushed the overflow
Of converse, as a cloud will still the songs
That rise from every copse, till Rukhmabai—
As one who dreams—began a tale of wrong
And wronging, such as clouds a myriad lives
Condemned to open their brown wistful eyes
Beneath the light of Indian suns—a tale?
Rather a passionless account of years

Terrible—strange, of a white soul alone
And warring with her world, a white strong soul
In whom the martyr spirit stood confessed.
And as the gentle accents rose and fell,
The turmoil of the city surged away
To leave us as two friends beneath the shade
Of waving palms, and with the murmurous hymn
Of ocean echoing round the rocky feet
Of Bombay, the sea-girt, the beautiful.

" Ere I had learnt to trust my baby feet
Across a room, the father that I knew
But as an arm that bore me to and fro,
Was plucked away—a green unready fruit
The wind had loosened, and I yet recall
The veil of tears that dimmed my mother's eyes
In those young happy half-remembered hours
Beneath the roof of Hurischundrajee,
My grandsire, the sweet mornings when I sat
Within the foolish shadow of a neem ;
And I yet faintly see the patient face,
That overwatched as the rich matron-moon
Would seem to note the wanderings of the stars.

" My parents were not of that holy caste—
Being not Brahmin but Kshatrya,
Whose widows, be they babe, or child or wife,
Must cut the lengthy tress and dwell accursed
As having by some sin in former lives
Brought death upon their husbands.   And of those

Who speaking with my grandsire stayed to woo
Was the physician Sakharam Arjun,
So patient-wise a lover, that the grief
Of a long faith but sanctified his love,
One who could wait until the falling tears
Were dried by ocean breezes, for we dwelt
Where the deep murmur of the Indian sea
For ever echoed in our ears, with song
Of all the goodly vessels that had sailed
To wealth and fame, and ne'er a dirgeful note
Of those who cumber the dead ocean-ground
With wrecks and slime and the white bones of men.
When the wan years had gathered seed and fruit
These seven times, since my young father passed
Into Nirvana's rest, Jayentibai
Who would no second wifehood, felt the strange
New pricking of a doubt.   What if her wish
To stay unwedded in her father's house
Were born of self?   And when the little doubt
Grew to a certainty, she bowed her head
Upon the offered love ; and with them, I
As a beloved daughter went.   We shared
A house with others of our class, a house,
Where six brave daughters filled the laughing air
With melody of bubbling song that wells
From happy youth in summer.   And my dreams—
For lonely childhood ever dreams—were filled
With wonder of new thought, as one who comes
Among a stranger-people, and is held
Uncertain, dwelling on their marvellous ways

And critical, but giving neither praise
Nor envious blame. For Hurischandrajee
Had held the orthodox and narrow creed,
Which later men, by stone and stone, have built
Upon the holy Vedas. He observed
All customs of our race, and thought them good
As given by Gods, who walked the earth in days
So dim, so far, the faintest star-world speck
Were nearer. But in this new home, the yoke
Of pale observances to which we set
No certain meaning, weighed but slenderly
On youth or age, and freedom was the note
To which the sitar of our life was tuned —
Not freedom for the men alone, but fresh
Untrammelled liberty for wife and maid
And every soul within the circling walls.
The women came and went, the maidens passed
To daily classes in the schools and stayed
Unwedded till their growth of happy years
Had bloomed thro' twelve red summers; while more
    strange
To one whose feet had trod the orthodox
Secluded path—they spake with bearded men
No veil about their beauty, and no sense
Of wrong to trouble the calm innocence
That sat enthroned in their deep-gazing eyes ;
And though my mother wondered, she was fain
To take her husband's judgment, seeing faults
In the old order and the new, yet glad
To recognise in this sweet liberty,

The tramp of serried thinkers who would win
Towards perfection.

"I was e'er a still
And sullen child, thinking my stir of thoughts,
Until the gloom and gold of fancy stretched
Beyond the merry circle, and I walked
In a dim solitude of dreams, to muse
On all the marvels of this newer world.
Behind me as a sunlit yesterday
Eight happy years lay dead.   Eight happy years?
Ay, happy tho' as stagnant as the pools
That in the jungle shadows lie concealed,
Dim years in which the utmost task of youth
Was to set grains of rice in little heaps
And mingle therein millet, white and brown,
Then patiently to sort the separate seeds.
A foolish waste of the hour-sands, a task
So tedious poor and worthless, that I thought
The sun must murmur as it sank away
Thro' the hot heavens 'Lost—a day—a life—
The life of every idler in the land.'
But the old indolence of orient life
Slumbered behind me, and a keener day
Was rousing all to effort, tho' I went
Not schoolways, being of a fearful mind
And well content to gather of the strange
New wisdom hovering on my father's lips ;
Which tho' not wholly understood, was drawn
Thro' memory into my very blood.

So in the rose-sweet garden of my youth
I wandered, gathered a bud, a deep
Hid golden heart, and later the red globe
Of hairy yellow seed—so lived and learnt.
Until the Brahmins named my wedding-day,
And the fair morning darkened as with cloud,
Wailing of waters and the hollow rush
Of a tempestuous wind.

                 " My father deemed
Our early marriages, the cankered fruit
Of a fair tree, and to the trembling joy
Of her he loved, withheld my passive youth
From thoughts of wedlock, till the eager years
Passing as bearers down the way, had brought
My dreamy steps unto the edge of ten.
And I, who saw the sad child-mothers laid
To early sleep, with weakly wailing babes
Profaning the dead silence of their rest,
Who watched them withering as stricken flowers
Which have no strength to broaden from their bud,
But linger, linger, till the browning leaves
Shrivel about their stem, would fain have stayed
For ever childless, husbandless, a trail
Of verdure clinging to its parent shade.
And hearing all they purposed I was moved
To conquer that shy reticence of speech,
Which ever hid the fancies of my heart ;
Crying : ' Oh must I wed?   Must every maid
Be mother ere she come to womanhood ?
Must I ?   The little Yasobai, who sat

Beside me but a score months ago,
Is dead to-day, and her still baby lies
Within her arms.   Oh, mother, let me stay
In this dear home unwedded.'   And tho' thick
Unwonted tears were gathering on the fringe
Of those deep eyes, she answered as in sad
And patient resignation, ' Little one ;
It was not Brahma's will, that any maid
Should keep her childish happiness.   We all
Must win to deeper life thro' pain, must grieve
To learn, and suffer to be purified.'
Meanwhile my father sought throughout the caste
For one in heart, and wealth, and lineage,
Worthy their leader's grandchild, but could find
No fitting youth, and in perplexity
Of half reproaches, grave unspoken blame
That he had thus delayed my marriage hour
Until too late, must hastily select
A youth of his own kindred, Dadajee,
Who tho' but poorly dowered, being son
Of a long-widowed mother, was content
To learn and labour till his diligence
Should build a home. 'And if,' they said, ' he takes
Our Rukhmabai to wife, he shall be trained
In all the wisdom of the schools, ourselves
Will find the necessary gold.'
                              " I heard
' The child shall wed with Dadajee,' yet spake
No word, but ran and hid myself and wept.
Not that I held my future lord in fear

Or loathing, having seen him now and then
About the house, and if I needs must wed
It little mattered who or what the man,
But that I dreaded marriage as the line
White line which would divide our sunny years
From the on-coming noons of cloud and grief.
And tho' I wept, it was in lonely hours,
For who would listen to a childish dread
And let it traverse all his ripened plans ?
And so in dull unspoken grief I saw
The last sweet golden weeks and days and hours
Slip madly by, as steeds that fly the rein,
Till on the latest evening as I dreamed
With weary lashes meeting, a wild dread
Possessed my soul, and roused me to a cry
Of ' Mother ! Mother ! must I pine and die
In that grim silence * which is laid on wives
In presence of their elders ?   I have heard—
Who has not ?—of the household cruelties,
To which the mothers of our husbands stoop
In blows and meagre food and ill report,
That they may come between us and the love
That had enriched our twilight, as with flush
Of the up-leaping sun—and surely death
Were softer than the cushions of a bride.

* An Indian girl is not allowed to speak in the presence of her elders, and as the new wife is generally the youngest person in the house, this rule is often very oppressive. One woman indeed assigned this unbearable silence as her only reason for attempting to commit suicide.

Oh, Mother! Mother! save me.'

                                    And she came
At that wild cry, soothing me in her arms
And murmuring: 'No silence for thee, child,
My first born, my beloved—no ill touch
Or word, or glance, no harsher hand than this ;
For he thou weddest, hath but scanty store
And could not find the daily milk and meat
For any household howsoever small.
So shalt thou aid me in domestic ways,
As elder daughter, till the lapsing years
Would call thy world-forgotten lily-life
To woman's duties.'   So my nearest dread
Was lifted, and with head upon that breast,
I sank again into the dreams of youth.

" The scent of jessamine was floating by
As tho' it wrapt the spirit of the breeze,
In viewless swathes of fragrance, when the five,
Who ever bathe the bride in water flushed
With turmeric came lightly thro' the rifts
Of silken curtain and disturbed my dreams—
Making the yellowed water stir and gleam
In the young light, until the dancing rounds
Flashed their reflection up the further wall
In silent laughter.   When the loathly bath
Which was repeated on successive morns,
Had left its staining yellows on my skin,
They steeped my hair in aromatic oils,
And loosened the rich spices, lingering

Until we heard the cadence of deep tones,
And knew that in the bird-world of fresh air
The priests were chanting, till the evil gods
Should flee the house.   When the fat offerings
Of butter, incense, money, betel-nuts
Rice and the concoo powder had been made,
Arthee performed, and the good gods invoked--
They came within, making an altar place
For the propitious images, with boughs
Of mango and about them heaping rice
And cocoa-nuts, with lamps whose dull red flames
Should linger till the shadows made them shine
As equals of the quick-forgotten sun.

"A robe of linen, yellowed dustily
With turmeric, was folded on the bride,
Who must abide within the doors, till eve
Had threaded the palm leaves with rosy light.
So stayed I by the altar, with dull blocks
Of deathly seeming, carven, staring, stiff
Before me as the likeness of my gods—
Not Brahma but a later thought, for men
Must create gods, as gods created men.
In the red afternoon, when sunset chill
Was thickening the soft and tender haze
That dwells about the May-world as a veil,
The women of our kindred would rejoice,
Sitting sedate about the laden boards,
And when the breezy shadows of the night
Laden with fragrance of dim roses stole

About the rooms, their comrades of the mart,
And camp, and city, gathered to make glad—
Feasting and holding wassail thro' the night.

"So ended the first day, but five were yet
To close before the marriage was complete
In all its ceremonial feasts and gifts.
On the succeeding morn the priests made known
The marriage-hour, and the musicians came
With treble flute, and the hoarse roll of drums ;
Seating them under the dark aisle of trees
Where widening crimson of pomegranate flowers,
With golden mohurs blazed upon the world
In tremulous deep bloom, a rain of dew,
As jewels yet upon their peachy breadth,
And the faint stir of breezes snatching stray
Sweet petals from above to strew the breast
Of the May-world, that as a bride was crowned
With budding jessamines.

                 "They plucked for me
Mograh and silee flowers, and knit the close
Fine stems into a chaplet for my hair,
When the deep yellow of the bath had dyed
My paler skin, and they would have me don
My father's gifts of gold and burning gems,
The nose ring of seven pearls, the silver bars
That chimed about my ankles.   And I stood,
Reluctant as a creature in the toils,
That views the glory of the outer world
Thro' mesh and bar, and shakes the net in vain.

" My mother's brother brought the marriage robe,
Silk saffron, and as soft as sheeny breast
Of the sun bird the knife, the cocoa-nut,
Gilded and to be left between my hands
All the long day, the luscious betel-leaves
And the two—nut and bulb—which should be tied
About my wrist to keep me from all spells
Of evil gods.   And once adorned, they brought
My slow unwilling feet unto the place
Of offering, and gave me rice to drop
In invocation, while the household went
To pray the bridegroom's presence, for the hour
Of sunset neared—the hour that was to link
Our separate lives in that unhappy bond.
In this fair isle, that as a mother soothes
Her sons with murmur of a hundred seas
And gentle beauty of low hills, the dales
For ever green and the rich pasturage
Deepening in fertile valleys—in this land
Of greater light, you have esteemed it sin
To wed without some growth of friendly love.
But we ?   What love is there between two babes
Who but obey the older stronger will ?
Two children, who are fain to run and play
When the dull ceremonies cease ?   I think
The freer is the nobler plan, more meet
For human dignity and that proud p.ace
We hold as in the front of time.

                              " They brought
My bridegroom thro' the busy sunlit streets,

                                        D

With music and due following of friends,
His horse slow-pacing, and upon his brow
The shining marriage jewel, while his lithe
Long fingers closed upon the string of beads
Which should adorn a wife.　They laid his gift
On my reluctant neck, giving my hand
Its trail of flowers, and seating us on grain
That one had gathered into heaps—yet held
A veil between our anxious eyes, and stayed
The great event.　I heard the busy priests
For ever chanting, chanting, till the bowl
Sank thro' the gleaming waters and the chant
Brake suddenly into triumphal sound,
The clash of music and the joyful beat
Of hands, with treble wailing of the flutes.
Then fell the veil, and my young husband stooped
Towards me with his beaded chain, while I
All timorously flung my fragrant wreath
About his neck, forcing the tear-drops back
And yielding my chill hand unto his clasp—
As unto clasp of Death.　They brought us forth,
To where the golden champacs were in flower,
Looming large on us as we drove away
Still side by side, but ever hushed and still,
As two wan children, set for punishment
Some task that overawes them as they work.

" So ebbed the marriage week, and I was free
To look again upon my mother's face
As wedded maid, to live the happy years

That were too golden to be long, in calm
Of studious labour, here an easy task,
And there a twilight frolic with the babes,
While the sweet mother-face, itself the law,
Must smile and smile, upon our foolish youth.

" But when I turned from the deep joys of home,
To learn and read and gather of the world—
Me-seemed the sorrows of surrounding lives,
In wrongs and poverty and lack of love,
Were of so vast a compass, that my heart
Was still within me, lest the burning prayers
I uttered might be, as a whisper lost
In city shouts.   The world that Brahma willed,
The world of palms, asokas gleaming pale,
And fragrant palsa-blooms—the world of waves,
Where delicate green fronds are lightly bowed
Beneath the wandering breezes, the live world
Of peoples, wise and many tongued, and sad
As the last echo of a tempest, cried
Thro' chants and mantras, offerings and prayers,
Up to the far Trimurti for redress
Of all its sorrows ; and I heard the deep
Half-stifled wail of millions as it rose
To echo in the all-wide ear of Brahm,
Until its rhythm was the only sound
Mine ears could hold, until it filled my days
With anguish and my very sleep with pain.
The maids who listened to my story-songs

Of the old Vedic days, when woman trod
The laughing earth as queen, who over-thought
My scanty store of books until the cloak
Of prejudice had fallen from their lives,
Were haled to wifehood, their reluctant feet
Beating sad measure in my dreams, and some
With weary, weary face of widowhood,
Turning the visions of my night to prayer.

" So dropped the years as a ripe flower that shakes
Its petals forth upon the amber air,
To swell about the hidden seed.   I read
Seeking the purer faith that Brahmos teach ; *
And storing all my second father's words,
As the pearl-seeker gathers every shell
That may contain a gem.

                              " Meanwhile the lad
My husband, left the even paths that bear
Towards an honourable age, for hours
Of spendthrift riot, till the punishment
Of evil ways befell his wasted frame,
And he went nigh to death.   A terror robbed
The hearts about me of their household peace
As one by one, like shadows when the night

* The Brama-Somaj, or Church of the Reformed Brahmins, is
the purest form of Theism, holding the same views as the Reformed
Jews and the Theists of Swallow Street, Piccadilly.

Is dewing the deep heaven with stars, the foul
And loathly stories crept into our ears ;
Stories so dark and terrible, I vowed
To spend my days in labour, loneliness,
Endure the utmost ill of mind or flesh,
Ere I would link my whiter life with one
So spotted and besmirched.   My father spake
His deep remonstrant word only to stir
A gust of passionate, disdainful wrath ;
So was enforced to sit with folded hands
And watch the gradual wrecking of his hopes.

" Meanwhile the lad, in whose had lain my hand
That wedding evening, lingered through the years,
Till three were numbered ; when new vigour stirred
His languid pulses and he rose and walked
The green earth in new life of feebleness ;
Yet did not ask my presence, had belike
Forgotten the dim ceremonial bond
That bound our lives.   As a dead history
Of bitter words and deeds, I can recall
When nineteen years had murmured in my ears
Their tale of numbered deeds and thoughts, a vague
Yet angry war anent the leadership
Of proud Kshatrya, our martial caste ;
A war that raged until its stony words
Had ground a rough and jagged enmity
To deadliest edge.   The spirit that would work
Another evil, finds the downward way
To be of soft descents, an easy road

Winding and winding over thymy turfs,
A upas-shadows here, the purple bloom
Of nightshade there.   But moving ever down
Through glade and glade, it loses the world-view,
The clear still light upon the mountain-heights
And the expanse of heaven, yet knows it not,
Having its eyes upon the slimy path
In search of weapons, and its mind so filled
With shadow, that the void of outer dark
Is but material image of its thought.
So those who sought to harass our repose,
Had searched but little, ere their cunning chanced
Upon a very poison-blade of ill—
I was not with my husband and if half
That rumour whispered of his life were true,
His claim must be the sorrow of my life,
Its one dark drop of ill.   'Twas easy then
To hold discourse, a cunning-shaped discourse
Of wifely wealth, desertion, and the rights
Of even the most unconsidered man—
Of even the most weak and vicious man,
Until the tool was sharpened for their work.
Enough that Dadajee was roused to send
And claim his wife ; and that I greeted those
Who came, with no denial or excuse,
Saving the question : ' Had he a fit place
For any woman, say a single room
And certainty of six rupees a month ?
I could not dwell with women of the stamp
Of those unfortunates, who made the roof

Which sheltered him, a byword and reproach.
And incensed at my calm reply, with stamp
Of angry feet upon the floor and threat
Of legal force, they hurried thence—alas
To put the threat in force, to file a case
Against us in the courts.

          " But ere the long
Delays were over, and the judgment given,
A slow breath ceased to leave me fatherless.

" My father died, and even as we wept,
The blank and unknown future stared us down
Into new fears, for his had been the hand
That aided me in walking the new ways
Of western thought, in claiming liberty
To break the contract that I had not willed ;
And others might believe the old was right,
And Infant Marriages which had begun
In stormy ages, when the Tartar chiefs
Where pouring their rough thousands over Ind,
More righteous than our fallible reforms.
So was I even as a startled child
That scarcely knows her fear, and yet is held
Unmoving, silent, till the light is brought,
And all the mighty shadows of the dark
Melt into nothingness. So with my dread !
For, moved by pity and a softened heart,
My grandsire laid a kindly wrinkled hand
Upon my head, and bade me strive or stay
As the white impulse of my womanhood

Should urge—and the fell shadows of my grief
Lessened a little, changing into hope
A tear-wet dream, through which the distant light
Was dimly visioned.
                    " In the weary days
Of loss and patience and still memory—
The silenced voice for ever in our ears,
And the dear step an echo in the dim
Death-shadowed rooms, I chanced upon the words
Of one * who strove to turn the seething tides
Of custom, and unloose the woman's bonds ;
A large and kindly soul that faced the storms
Of adverse prejudices with such a front
Of steadfast calm as Buddha may have worn.
And shaking off the shackles of distrust
Which had confined my utterance to the small
Kind world of home, I penned a burning cry,†
The wrongs of my dumb sisters given sound,
And set before the world—a cry of pain,
Wailing and wailing thro' our Indian night,
So dark a night that tho' the western wealth
Of freedom give us rule, altho' the lights
Of far free centuries shine dimly down
The ages, we must ever turn and turn
In shadow and the shine of fainting stars.

* Mr. Behramji Malabari.
† Letter on infant marriages and enforced widowhood, which appeared in the *Times* of India, and for whose irreproachable English, Rukhmabai was indebted to the kindly correction of a friend.

" Upon the very morn my case was tried —
And Justice Pinhey stigmatised the will
To overbear a chill reluctant maid
As barbarous—that chronicle of wrongs
With which I thought to stir a lion's sleep,
My letter—filled the columns of the press,
Was answered, praised, reviled : " A woman's heart
Throbs thro' the earnest pleading." " We insist
The style is masculine, a woman's pen
Had never such a boldness ; " and my words
Vibrating thro' the land, were echoed back
By every journal, till they crossed the seas,
And called, thro' the wide columns of the *Times*,
Upon a greater multitude than that
Which rules our India.

        " Dadajee appealed,
And once, twice, three times, in as many years,
The verdicts ran, the balance of the law
Inclining now on his side, now on mine,
But latterly, without a break, on his ;
So that my little world of kindly souls,
Indian and English, drew more anxious breath,
As fearing for me the blank prison walls.
But what were months of durance to a life
Of loathèd wifehood ? What the prison air,
To that which stagnates in our narrow rooms
Behind the purdah ? And meanwhile the man—
(Whom I had thought to honour in old times
When the new marriage-bond but lightly bound
My spirit, and the flowers of hope were red,

A loose and careless blossoming of rich
Rose-petals nodding, nodding in the sun)—
Must pour a printed lie into the world,
A lie to blacken my dead father's name,
A lie—a creeping evil—and as such
I blazoned it ; and when their baffled rage
Drew me before the judge, he left the lie
With those who spake it, and I came again,
Altho' the people cursed me as I came.

" Upon the next appeal I was condemned
To join my husband, or be shut away
In prison for the space of half a year—
To join this husband who might wed again,
Divorce this wife or that, love here, love there,
And sin against us.   Remedy ?   Divorce ?
Alas ! the only remedy is death.
And to such pass is womanhood betrayed,
By the new law that England has been pleased
To graft upon the laws of Manu—Law ?
If it be law to re-stitute a right
That knew no institution.   One appeal
Remained to my unwearied band—a suit *
Which should be tried in England ; but the men
Who wrought against us feared the sympathy
Which would look richly out of English eyes,
And offered to forego their specious claims
For a consideration of rupees—

* Before the Privy Council.

Red gold in lieu of a reluctant wife.
And those about me urged the compromise
On my reluctant will, till at the last
I yielded—to repent before the day
Had gathered in its sheaves of light.   The law
Was stayed, but that decisive 'yea' or 'nay'
Which should determine the uncertain fate
Of generations yet to come, remains
A space unspoken.   Better I had borne
The pain of durance—ay, and greater pains —
If by so doing I had roused the world
Into repression of old usages,
Which, cursing the sad mothers of our race,
Recoil upon their children.   I would die,
If this poor life could buy repeal of laws
Unjust—unworthy of this England's fame ;
Could purge the statute-book of these decrees,
Which bear upon the.lives of maid and wife,
As an intangible dull weight."
                                        But I
Who felt the throb of earnest English life,
And loved the mighty mother, must upraise
Protesting voice, as one who should maintain
Her honour against all the world.   " Such law,
Had it not reason, were a grievous stain
Upon the justice of our rule, yet men
Will worship divers gods, and we would give
Brahmin and Buddhists—ay, and Mussulman—
The utmost liberty of faith.   I think
The grievances of women must be due

To precepts of their creed, rites that our law,
Respecting the dim faiths of every folk,
Would fear to touch, rites which must fade away
Thro' wear of time and growth of younger creeds."

"Ah, say you so?   And yet the Shastras fix
The time for marriage, at that age of youth
Which holds a maid upon the dreamy edge
Of her ripe womanhood, and would that lads
Should close their prentice-years of studentship,
Before they take the burdens of full life
Upon their strength.   And if this victor land
Refuse to tamper with a people's faith,
Why was the Juggernaut procession stayed,
Suttee forbidden and infanticide—
The death of the unwelcome, made a crime?
This breadth of love and judgment that can bear
With every harmless superstitious rite—
Were worthy of your England, but her heart
Should rise in mother-protest to forbid
The bitter woman-martyrdom, that fills
Our heavenward space with its despairing cry.
Nor do we ask a rough subversive change,
But merely that you should not force a maid
To ratify the contract that was framed
In her unconscious youth, that you should pass
A law enabling parents to delay
The marriage age, and leaving one who takes
A second spouse, the money that was hers
By her first husband's will.   Merely to aid,

By standing still, where hitherto your hands
Have pushed us onward ; by slight shift of law
To ease our burdens, not so great a change
Save in its meaning to the numberless
Pale women weeping behind purdah-silk.
Let England rise in her old strength and strike
As Mother of Free Nations at the laws
Which lay our millions in the jewelled dust
Of crumbled empires and dead usages.
The stern responsibility is laid
If 'duty must be measured by our powers'
On the broad shoulders of the ruling race.

"We ask our human rights ; the liberty
Of marriage contract ; the long rights of babes
Now taken, given, stolen, but of which
The law is guardian, here, ay and with us ;
The right of justice even if we be
But women, for tho' India is afar
Justice is Justice over all the world.

"And you?" I asked, leaving the mighty cause
For smaller detail, as we leave the moon
To mark the glowworm's tremulous green spark.

"Some of your earnest English gave me help,
Their countenance, sweet leisure and a home.
And one * who loved our common womanhood—

* Mrs. Eva McLaren.

Ay, all who bear the burdens of that name,
The burdens and the glory, without let
Of creed or class or country, called me thence
To rest upon her wondrous mother-love,
That spark of the divine which lifts our sex
Above its fellow and if great in her
Who spends it upon clustered golden heads,
How far more great in those who fold their arms
About the helpless children of a world.

"To give love worthily, and find it grow
Thro' glorious years until the cause is won—
The wife and husband walking as true mates
Towards the far event—my friend's deep hope
A hope in part fulfilled. And I who heard
Her clear voice calling thro' the storm, arose
Crossing the turbulent high wave, and now
Would learn all doctor-lore, that I may go
Again to those who need me, may rejoice
My mother's heart and heal the sick and sad,
So labour till the fulness of my days
Has lifted me into Nirvana's calm."

And as I plunged into the outer whirl
Of our unresting London, a rich dream,
The optimistic and utopian hope
Thrilled thro' the troubled turmoil of my thought ;
Till I beheld an age when broader minds
Should sway the people's sceptre, statesmen seek
Not so much the advancement of their land

In the world's eye, but in the eye of God.
As the dim centuries roll out of time,
Their hopes and aspirations are a lamp
To guide us thro' the twilight, till we near
The throne of His perfection and look deep,
Thro' veils and mists into the shining light
Of day that shall be ; wherefore then the fears
That hold us back from any daring good ?
The day must break, and every step we take
Towards the east shall bring us nearer dawn ;
What matter then if all the onward way
Be set with flints, and but our children live
To reach the morning-land ?   To-day is ours,
A space whereon to write our works in fair
Bold lettering, or the hasty scrawl of fear ;
A space which shall go down the countless years
To bear us record.
                          Oh ye woman-hearts
Who are the strong salvation of our land,
Let the deep sorrows of a kindred race,
Sprung with our own from the old Aryan home,
Awaken you to burning thought and speech,
Till the pathetic echo of your tones
Has made the weakest strong, the strongest sad ;
Till English millions send a rousing cheer
Across the sea and the child-wife is saved,
The widow—one wife of one spouse—set free
To wed in honour, and our India's wound
An anguish of the past.

[When Conrad III. was in 1138 proclaimed Emperor of Germany, the Duke of Wittenberg refused to acknowledge him as such. The Emperor therefore besieged the Duke, who had taken refuge in his fortified town of Weinsberg. The Duke in the end was forced to yield ; whereupon the indignant Emperor declared his intention of putting all to fire and sword, but granted permission to the women to depart in safety, and to carry with them whatever they regarded as most precious. The Duchess of Wittenberg, taking advantage of this concession, with ready wit took her husband, the Duke, upon her back. Her example was followed by the other women ; and the Emperor, seeing them thus come out with the Duchess at their head, was touched by the spectacle, and pardoned the men for the sake of their wives.]

THEY are hushed—the hoarse voices of battle,
    The clashing of shields,
For at sundown, despairing of succour,
    The proud city yields.
Then fill me the ruby-red beaker
    Brim-high at the spring ;
To-morrow we drink amid plenty
    ' Wass-hael ! ' to the king !

Oh, sweeter than toil of the bondsman.
    Than hawking of lord,
Is the snort of the earth-spurning charger,
    The play of the sword.

What, ho ! are they pleading for mercy,
    The treacherous foe ?
Shall we listen with many a brother
    Laid silent and low ?
Nay, nay ; let the women and children
    Go forth with their best
Of jewels and house-gear and linen—
    Short shrift for the rest.
Oh, sweeter than toil of the bondsman,
    Than hawking of lord,
Is the snort of the foam-whitened charger,
    The play of the sword.

They come—over-burdened, I warrant,
    With treasurings rare ;
Wives, mothers, and matrons—by Odin !
    'Tis men that they bear.
" Have mercy, O army victorious !
    You bid us go free,
With the gold and the gems that we value,
    The babes at our knee ;
But dearer than house and the children,
    Wherever we roam,
Are the treasures we bear on our shoulders,
    The shields of the home."

E

" There are wives by the strand of the ocean,
　　And maidens as fair,
Who weep through the whir of the spinning,
　　And shield us with prayer ;
For the sake of those watching and waiting
　　Afar by the sea,
For the love and the faith of the women,
　　Pass on—ye are free ! "
Oh, sweeter than carnage and glory,
　　Than jewels and gauds,
Is the neigh of the home-coming charger,
　　The sheathing of swords.

A WOMAN'S VENGEANCE

My cottage—mine ! I pace the earthen floor
Seven paces either way, and count the steps
From hearth to threshold, from the white array
Of household ware, to yonder western panes.
The veriest hovel—dark and damp and dull,
Is some dim soul's ideal of a nest
Wherein to rear its young—a nest, a home,
A wall about the sacredness of life,
As the warm flesh is set between our souls
And the world-eye.   Before my latching door,
Some feet of sward and waving bloomy growth—
A clump of lilies and the golden globe
Of a faint evening primrose, where the rich
Rayed sunflower nods throughout the drowsy noon,
With further the wild hyacinth, and dusk
Of pansies under shelter of the hedge—
Some feet of sweet and scented garden earth
Slope to the little gate beneath the limes ;
The little gate whereon in twilight hours
I lean a-weary, the o'er-busy day
Remembered but as winter, when the sun

Is browning the rich yellows of the wheat,
While chatter of brown house-holds, lightly rocked
In the leaf-darkness over-head, grows faint,
A murmur and a silence, a low note
And the swift flutter of belated wings.
The land is mine, a space of God's good earth,
A quarter of an acre and a house !
And mine by honest labour, mine to hold
Until the dulness of old age shall shut
The glint of sunlight on a pansy heart,
The thrush's liquid song, the scent of thyme
Out of my knowledge—and the twilight hush
Deepen into the drowsy night of death.

A breeze has wakened and the lily-heads
Tremble upon their stems, a cool sweet breath
That murmurs of the kine, kneedeep in grass
Beyond the river, of the flags and reeds
That rustle o'er its slaty gleam.   The light
On yonder plain is still as golden pure
As when the mammoth feasted on its low
And watery levels, the pale glow of blue—
An opal steadied, shines as faintly clear
As ever before thronging human feet
Brake through the darkness of primeval Time,
To soil the springing sweetness of the meads
With brick and stone and staring window-eye.
But we, who gather memories of sweet
And bitter, as two flowers on a stalk,
Must leave our youth before its red and white

Of chestnut bloom be driven from our cheeks.
We age betimes, when death and falsehood keep,
By turn and turn, the watches of the night ;
We age betimes when a long summer drought
Follows upon the spring-time of our love,
And faith be withered in the heated noons.
So am I old, who loved in innocent
May-glooms, who loved to lose, and see the dark
And purple poison-flower burst the sheath
That should have held a lily—hate for love.
Oh, heart ! the growth is fine, the flower is fair !
Lily or nightshade—he who sowed the seed
Shall pluck the fruit !

                The year—that dreamy space
Of golden morns and noons that brought the dream—
Alas, no more !—of an abiding love
Into my life, was one of rain and sun ;
A shower, a smile, and every day a shower
With after sun, until the oat was ripe,
Or ever the green stem had yellowed fair
Into the rustling straw.   But ere the lights
Of rosebud May had broadened into suns,
And yet the grass was waving in the deep
Rich water-meadows, through the village street
With cant of poverty on artist-lips,
A painter wandered ; one who sketched his home
As a dull attic in a London street,
And spake of early struggles ; yet who heard
" Sir Wilfred " from the world, and knew no more

Of stinted bread than the dull sovereign
Who dreams himself a beggar. Had we heard
Of rank that needs must wear the ploughman's shirt
To gain a happy hour, we should have smiled
As wise grey fathers when the children talk.
Happy? the poor? No prince of long descent
Would lift the golden circlet from his brow
For any hope of happiness in toil,
For any hope of comfort in the loss
Of cleanly ways, of delicate desires,
And all that makes existence sweet and fair
To souls of gentle breeding. So the plea
Of broken health and poverty sufficed ;
And Wilfred set his easel in the room
Low-browed and white, and sweet with lavender,
That overlooked the thymy common-land ;
A painter who could sketch our gentle hills,
The blacksmith in his cavern, and the bench
Beside the ancient alehouse, that could show
A wondrous passage under earth, and gloom
Of deep unhappy dungeons. He must aid
In stacking, threshing the rich sheaves, and stand
Beside my bin, as browning fingers pulled
Its dusty golden treasure from the bine,
For ever plucking, plucking, till the soft
Rich hillock rose upon the canvas sides.

And when I glanced from all the busy world
Of autumn to the shadows of the brush,
In deepening colour laid upon the white

Snow-stretch of canvas, I must ever find
A face familiar—dusky-eyed and ripe,
With cloud of crisp, rebellious hair, and lips
A ruddy—all the pool had flashed me back
Since first I looked into its depths and laughed.
For though none other than a farmer's child,
I think—I *know*—that I was all as fair
As any born to ermine of a throne—
Their all ; for mark you, queen and serving-maid
Are simply women in the thoughts of God.
Fair ?   Ay, accursed with beauty, which had been
The dower of richer women, but in me
Seemed a presumption.   Beauty should be born
To the maid-children of more leisured thought
Than that which delves and spins.   A farmer's child ?
Then give her, for all dower, an honest face—
An honest breadth of face—with flush of health
Beneath the browning kisses of the sun.
More beauty were presumption—ay, a lure
Of Satan, rather than a gift of God ;
A lure to catch the eye of gentle blood,
And stoop it to a wedlock out of place.

Can love be out of place ? when human blood
Would claim a kinship with the breathing wrongs
Of half a world, and when the ancestry
Of peer and peasant started from the soil
As brothers, in the yesterday of time ?
What is this gentle blood ?   The pride of wealth,
A little more refinement in the blood,

A little greater knowledge of the small
Pale lies that fall as oil upon the wheels
Of social life ?   And love of meeting souls ?
I am a simple woman ; but I think
The earnest love of man and womanhood
A something holy—something over earth,
And chance, and all that lower men would find
In its impassioned mystery.

                     Through all
The morrows of a sweet rain-heavy June,
When every blue-bell in the woods was hung
So thick with dew, it drooped anigh the earth
As though to lay its sorrows on the breast
Of the Eternal Mother, Wilfred stayed,
Painting and dreaming ; a rich breath of song,
A zither, and a voice that called me fair,
More fair than all the cultivated blooms
That shake their heavy petals in the breeze—
A stray wild rose, that glorified the hedge
Of bramble, nettle, bracken, and was touched
With the soft blushes of departing day.
What wonder that I listened—that I loved ?
A painter—poor ; a gentleman—the name
Gave a traditionary ring of worth,
As when we strike a healthy round of gold
Upon the board.   What wonder that I deemed
The artist-soul, behind those slumb'rous deeps,
As honest as the labourer's in the field ?
More honest, being born to noble thoughts

Of a fair mother, who had taught his lips
Their infant prayer of love and penitence,
While yet the merest words were sweet and strange.
What wonder that I gave a simple faith,
And found it only wonderful and sweet
That I, a sweet-leaved briar of the hedge,
Was chosen, while the stately lilies bloomed
In glistening purity and—bloomed alone.
I, a poor rose, that he must prune and train,
Until its briars should o'errun the home
With buds and widening flowers and scented leaf.
I was young then—so young that I must sing
Morn in and through the noontide, until eve
Was washing the red sunset from the deeps
Of darkening space.   I was young then, too young
To comprehend the stirless hot-house pride,
Which looks through windows on our common earth,
And holds aloof, ay, verily, is proud
Of folded hands ; yet with an equal pride
I churned the cream until a golden heap
Of butter lifted from the thinner milk ;
And truest pride—if pride at all be true—
Must sooner rest with those who earn a meed,
Than with the silken soul whose idleness
Was purchased by ancestral toil or fraud—
Or fraud ? belike, for fortunes can be built
Upon the lives of poorer men—be forced
From failing hearts and houses, the red gold,
The *blood*-red gold.   Alas ! the wisest rogue
Heaps to himself the riches of the earth,

While honesty goes barefoot all the day—
The little day of this imperfect life.

For all the merry thoughtlessness of youth,
I had o'erthought the future, a few springs
Of freedom—a long courtship in the lanes—
Laborious noons, and a long dreamy eve,
With old hands resting on the elbowed chair,
And old dim eyes regarding the fair heads
Of children's children.

     A sweet hope—a dream!
Alas, that all the fairest in our thought
Should yield to time and—as the emerald light
Of glow-worms fading, leaves a worm indeed—
Be all the darker for the sometime glow
Of a dead hope. The rustic wooer came,
As in my school-girl thought—a man of worth,
With farm and homestead and a hundred kine.
An honest man and loving, one whose hand
Would have held mine in faith of wedded life
Thro' all the years. But Wilfred flashed a smile—
Thro' the mist-morning of my maiden dreams,
And rougher honesty was overpassed
For then—and for all time. For who can heed
The cry of corncrakes, when a nightingale
Is flooding the dim world with song? Alas,
Not I, who listened till the music sank
Into my soul,

    —till a low echo woke
To give again the rapture of its trills,
And I—I loved.

                    The harvesters' ripe moon
Was waning tenderly as down the paths
We strayed in converse or sweet silences,
Until the last dim evening.   He had drawn
My hands into his keeping ere we paused
To lean upon the stone-work, lichen grey,
Of the old fountain.   A neglected briar
Was leaning its last bud upon the edge
Of the smooth round, a white thing, mirrored fair
In the still stretch beneath our gazing eyes.
And to our hearts the silence of the night
Had brought a sudden wistful tenderness,
For tho' content with love, a doubt, a dread—
Foolish as fancy of a bead of cork
In wine of clear and bubbling gold, had roused
The vague disquiet of too happy hours ;
Till in a tremulous dismay I clung
Yet closer to his arm—ah me, and heard
Only the echo of my fears.   "Alas
That clouds must overcast our love, and bring
The winds of winter swirling thro' the boughs
Of every green retreat, but men must eat.
And if I will to line our city nest,
I needs must labour till the dreary yoke
Of winter has been lifted from the land.
But trust me child, and I will come again,
Ere yonder clump of sleeping lilies turn
A widening petal to the sun."

                    I broke
Into quick sobs : " You will not come again ;

Some mist will come between us—oh, I know—
You love me—and such love as ours can stretch
From world to world, from age to age—nor change
Tho' all the persecutions of ill-fate
Should overwash its patience, yet I fear—
Some woman-instinct lifts a warning hand,
And if we part to-night——"

                      He bent his lips
To mine, as tenderly as when we pledged
Our love in the dim stillness of the woods,
Where the brown needles of forgotten years
Deadened the steps. "And if we part to-night,
The love that has detained my wandering feet
These many months will turn them hitherward,
Whatever lion venture to contest
The backward path." So held me close and went
As must all good, all evil when the wheel
Of fate has turned.

                  The ruddy leafage died,
And starlings thronged the mead, a whirl of snow
Whitened the thymy common, and lay deep
Upon the further hills, but sunny dreams
Were in my heart, until a rumour fell
As sudden winter on my life. "A poor
And struggling artist, who for daily bread
Must sketch and sell and sketch? A likely tale
When all the county knows of Wilfred Burne—
Sir Wilfred—since his father's death—a man
Eccentric if you will but true of heart,

A Woman's Vengeance

And to be wedded ere the close of June
To an Earl's daughter—Lady Agatha."

So, like the sudden fading of a haze
My dream dissolved, and I was left to face
The wide grey prospect of a desolate
Unhappy day.   But when my father came
From market with the rumour on his lips
I heard and smiled, pouring the home-brewed ale
With strung still hand, until the father-thought
Was all content.   " My lass can hold her own
With any of your gilded gentlefolks."
For with a bubbling laughter on my lips
I echoed back, "A wedding did you say?
I trust he will invite us to the feast.
You to the tenants' dinner, I to join
Light-heart, light-foot in every mazy dance."
But tho' I smiled, it was as one who hides
A darkness in her thought—as the still pool
May glitter golden in the morning light,
Altho' the dead are tangled in its weed.

Oh death of love that leaves an after pain
For time to heal! Alas that manhood's vows,
Tho' strongly told, and bound about with hopes
That shine as jewels in the morning sun,
Should be but as an arm-thick rope—of sand—
A rope that crumbles into pitiful
Poor dust, before the hand has stirred its coils.
And yet my heart, the longest day is lived,

And dull to-morrows steal our very hurts,
Till all that has been, seems but as a cloud
Across the noon-tide sun.

                 When New Year frosts
Were leafing all the panes, Sir Wilfred sent
A jewel with his love—a golden round
Whose eastern over-pearling closed in fire
Beneath the hot eye-rubies of a snake ;
A jewel—and a page of pale regrets :—
" For all his love, he might not hold my youth
To a long waiting upon fortune's tide
When worthier men "—from first to last a lie !
The lie of one who set the world's regard
In the high places of his soul, and deemed
It out of nature that a gentleman
Should need to give account of all his works ;
Should—even when divested of his silk
And purple by the hand of death—descend
To the dull level of ignoble folks.

A lie ! and with no poor imprudent hint
Of whence it came, beyond the London mark
Upon the cover, lest in love or hate
I should pursue him—I ! who was as proud
As ever royal dame, too proud to more
Than close the jewel in its velvet case,
And send it back without a written word,
Save and except the outer name—the name
And title that he fancied unconfessed !

Oh false and fickle heart of man!   Have all
Who bear them proudly under that poor name
So small a power of loving? is all faith—
In man—a virtue of so rare a growth,
That it were well, if woman ever deemed
Her lover false, till time had proved him true?
Alas the slighter vessel, soonest heats,
And that slow love of womanhood that grows
About the man and house to warm a life,
Can only hope a year-long passion-gleam
In answer, the hot flash of bursting light
That leaps and sinks, and sinking fades away,
As utterly forgotten as the breeze
That fanned our foreheads on the yester-eve.

When spring returned to scatter thro' the woods,
Her wealth of pale unscented flowers, and fair
In every meadow hung the cowslip heads,'
My father went into the fields at dawn—
A man in the brave autumn of his years,
Yet who must tell them over in the grave
Before a week was added.   Two and two
The tramp of heavy feet upon the flags
Smote on my heart and as I turned, behold
I knew the secret of that hurdle-couch,
That four strong men were bearing tenderly
Across the little yard beyond the door.
I knew—and had no need of faltered words
To tell me that my father was asleep,

With mystery of slumber in a smile
That should not change until the trump of doom.

So was I loosed from every tie of love
That I would suffer ; for the patient soul
Who waited—waited—and must win reply
To a renewed petition, in the hour
When I was saddest and most lonely, found
An equal faith that set against his wish.
" Love, marriage, children, home ?   I rather choose
The solitary way, and will to learn
That learning I may serve."   So went my way
To the great city with its drowning deeps—
Its million hurrying feet that beat the wall
Of the down-trodden into triumph-songs,
To learn of nursing in the orderly
Long wards of a grim hospital—-to learn,
And watch, and serve, and after patient years
Be lent to yonder black unlovely town.
I work—the past if not a folded page,
At least concealed beneath the press of small
Sufficient duties, as a desert death
Is hidden by the shifting flow of sand.
I work and wait, knowing that all things come
To an exceeding patience.   Love is long,
Longer than life, and hatred as its twin—
Day light and dark, can mock at time and chance,
In a long day which overpasses death
And triumphs in the grave.

I was a maid
As innocent as any nursling child,
When Wilfred cast the shadow of his love
Across the stir and purpose of my day.
I should have been a happy wife—thank Heaven
My hands are strong to labour, I am free
To wed or work, and need not take the home
And the man with it, from desire of bread,
As many a hapless creature who is rocked
In jewelled cradle.   Had Sir Wilfred loved
For but one heart-beat—one—I had forgiven.
But even while he wooed me with low words
His heart was hers, and this will I requite.
I think we women were not served so ill,
If vengeance, swift or slow, but ever sure
Waited upon the wronger.
                              Hist—a step !
So like it is, I almost hear the cry
Of the loose gravel by the farmhouse door,
As when he came a-weary from the fields.
He ?   But I dream, and dreams have set the sweet
Sad echoes of the olden time afloat.
Yet—Oh my God ! had ever living man
As proud a step, as that which strikes the flag
Beyond my door, such passionate deep eyes,
With such a glitter of rebellious hair
Above the azure gleam.   It cannot be—
That he for whom I wait throughout the long,
Long years, should chance upon my latching door,
And yet—and yet—

F

Oh Lord mine hour is come,
And Thou hast given me my heart's desire !

"The district nurse ? Joan—you ! I—pardon me."

"What is your pleasure ?   I am here to serve."

And in an eagerness that overpassed
The momentary wonder ; for a grief
New born and fierce, is more than memory,
He cried : "And for such service am I come."

" To one," I answered, with a little smile,
Malicious, cold, " who owes you a long debt
And will be proud to pay it—love for love."

"A debt ?"

　　　　　"Ay so, the debt of culture.   I
Was but a farmer's daughter, with some skill
Of labouring hands, but strangely ignorant
Of many a poet's love-sick rhapsody,
Until Sir Wilfred sang.   Books, pictures, prints—
Somewhat of science, more of artist-lore
I gathered from his lips, and have besides
To thank him for my knowledge of the faith
And honour that is closed in gentle blood.
What is your need ?   The Lady Agatha
Perchance has found a restless hour or two
In her full sheaf of poppy-headed nights ?"
But in the gravity of reasoned fears,

He let my bitterness, as something strange,
Not pertinent, slip by him and be lost.
"The past is dead, as any autumn leaf
That hurries thro' the stormwind of the north ;
And you whose heart was ever woman-warm,
Will scarcely turn from childhood's agony
Because the father sinned.   My child ; and left
To toss in lonely fever ; for an ill
Of loathsome dens, has rasped her lily skin
And mother—maids—— Can no affection bear
The strains of time and sickness ?   I am mad
With a destroying terror, and my lips
Would pour the bitterness which they have drawn
From one chill life, upon the greater hearts
Which teach us in their mother-care, of love
Beyond this human.   Bear with me—the child—— "

" Your child ?"

                   " My only child."

                             " The Lord be praised :
Blessed be He who hath maintained my cause,
Who hath delivered them that hated me
Into mine hand !"

                        " That you may compensate
Your soul for an old wrong, with coals of fire."

" So spake the Christ, but royal singers poured
The will of God in wilder strains of song ;
And I—I follow David.   You forget ?

Ah well, your soul's salvation is not set
Upon the Hebrew Psalms.   But now—your child ?

" Ay—mine, the rosebud of a thorny stem
That one dark morning looked upon the light,
And since has seemed the one flower among leaves,
A stray white blossom, that in innocence
Smiled on a garden-world of hidden thorns—
The sharp beginning, ay, the all of life,
For since our summer idyll——— "

                              " You profane
A memory that should be mine alone—
My Eden.   Innocence ?   Had I not been
So childlike, I had doubted.   Idyll ?   Ay
If lies may be idyllic.   Oh false heart
How had we wronged you that you should repay
Our welcome—the rich welcome of the poor—
With such a poor concealment of your rank—
Your name—your wealth—with such a feigned
        regard,
From dawn to dusk the living of a lie.
Forgive me, if in my unpolished speech,
The little necessary slip be termed
A lie—no less—and sport of hearts, such sport
As breaks a woman's heart in the result—
Unmanliness.   Oh Wilfred, are the streams
Of human love so many and so near,
That you can start them with a grinded heel,
Drink of the bubbling waters and so pass ? "

" Joan—Joan. My little love, my briar rose,
So sweet, so fresh, so innocent, I loved—
But deemed it were the nobler part of love
To leave you, tho' I hungered for your face
And heard your sweet voice singing thro' the hours,
And singing ever to a broken song,
In which a sorrow throbbed with the delight—
As in dim twilights the hid nightingale
Murm'ring of love must tune her note to pain.
But sweet believe me, tho' her liquid song
Bring every bird about her feet, she were
More happy mated with a nightingale,
Than if she turned unto an eagle's love.
Her slender wings should spread in woodland flight,
Her song——"

        I broke across the specious words
With simple truth : " If eagles may not wed
With lesser fowl, they should not stoop to woo."

" I grant it sweet, but beauty such as yours—
A rose among the brambles of the hedge,
Must bow the wisest to a reverence
And some-time worship."

        " Worship and not love :
Dear heart, how wise in specious sophistry
Of self-excuse, are cultured gentlemen !
Sweet reverence and worship such as kings
May yield a loveliness of heaven, is pale
As moonlight, after the red light of day

Has blazed a pathway down the western skies ;
And love—the love you pledged in woodland dusk
Beneath the ranking firs, as far outshines
That ecstasy of worship, as the fires
In yonder furnaces my kitchen spark.
But punishment awaits the broken oath
As certainly as darkness follows day."

A shadow fell and deepened in the blue
Of those uplifted eyes. " Love—punishment :
God knows my slender debt of broken faith
Was paid, and overpaid, and paid again,
By the dull fate that turns our dearest hope
Into a dead-sea apple, ere it reach
The destined lips."

                    "You married where you would,"
And the deep passion of embittered love
Burned in my speech : "a lady fair as dawn ;
So fair the rougher winds and rain of heaven
May never touch the lily of her throat,
Or burn on those red-petal lips ; so fair
So wealthy, and of such a high descent,
It was an equal wedding when she loved
Sir Wilfred Burne—an honourable man
Of stainless record, one whose constancy
A lengthy year had proven.   Punishment ?
That is to come."

                    " I married where I would :
A woman whom my lover-dreams had raised

To a dim eminence of angelhood.
I married where I would, alas to find
A coldness of perennial frost, that knew
No leaping spirit-throb of love or life.
A happy man?   So happy, that the fiend
Is ever pouring the red wine, with chink
Of gold in little heaps about the board,
While thro' my thought, the whisper rises ' Drink.
Drink deep and play, till dull forgetfulness
Has sealed the brain, or deeper drink and — die.'
But baby hands have beat the tempter back
And baby-laughter, as a thrush's note
After long rain, has raised a trembling hope,
A hope, a dream——"

                    "And now the child shall die."
I spake it hardly, clearly, and the ring
Of the slow words was as the fall of steel ;
Altho' my heart misgave me, for the love
Of children lay a-warm about my thought.
" I am the only woman far or near
That fears not death, nor this most loathsome ill,
And I would sooner slay myself, than lift
A finger to delay the hurrying feet
Of him who robs us of our pain in sleep,
A long, long sleep, Sir Wilfred.   What? is sin
To be forgotten in the hour of need ?
Is that long ruthless lie to be forgiven ?
I think not.   You have wrought against my life,
And now for all your wealth and poet-lore,

For all the artist cunning of your touch,
The child must die untended. You may charm
The whole wide world and yet be powerless
To disarm death.

         Go back, thou lying soul,
Fiend-set in such a shape, go, watch the stir
Of limbs and lips, until her latest breath
Has quivered out upon the night—the ear
Can have too few of even fevered words."

"You have no mercy?"

         " None."

         A dull despair
Was pressing out the faint and fevered hope,
Yet he must turn within the door to urge
A thought upon me : "Can no memory
Of woodland strolls beneath the ripening nuts,
With lengthy grasses swaying in the breeze
And a long bramble catching at your robe,
Of hours wherein at least we were content—
Can no such memory disturb your will?
I can recall an evening when you swore
The hardest task were as a little sleep—
The languid dreaming of an hour, when wrought,
Begun, and ended, for the tender sake
Of one beloved."

         " Beloved ? Oh ay ; but love
And I are strangers ; yet if this poor babe
Had been the child of other——"

         " Spare me that.

" The child of other than Sir Wilfred Burne
I had not dallied thus."

                He put a hand
Unto his heated brow and turned away :
" Alas ! my little Joan, that thou shouldst pay
The forfeit of thy father's sin ; that guilt
Should be washed out in blood of innocence."
And as he passed me, with a staggering step
That sought the door, I caught at the lax hand.
" You called her Joan ? "

              A bitter accent leapt
Into the husky and despairing voice.
" Ay, the chill loveliness of marble brings
A pang of longing for those warmer arms,
That clasped and clung in the hey-day of youth.
But let me pass, the wailing of a child
Is in my ear and I forget the past,
Love—pleasure—all.   The child, and there is none
To moisten her parched lips, to give her air,
Oh God, the child ! "

            I was of woman born,
And in my time had felt the warmth of love
Yield unto creeping of a chill despair ;
I was of woman born, and loving once
For all the loosened bitterness and pain
Of a dark hour, must share his passing thought,
His anguish, tho' a cruel wrong was walled,
As heaven-high, between our meeting hands.

"The child, the little Joan; oh, Wilfred, stay
That I may overthink the grievous pass
In which I stand—the vengeance that I vowed
Before me, and the need of such a one —
A babe, a little helpless dying child
Beyond my door. Stay then," and to and fro
I paced in wildered thought, until a wave
Of dim emotion rolled across my soul,
And I was fain to seek the freshening cool
And silence of the flower-guarded gloam.
How starry-pale the lilies are in dusk
Of an approaching night; and lo, a bud
Is broken from the rose-tree, such a bud
As blossoms in Sir Wilfred's life. Poor babe!
The mother-love which should have ministered
Unto thy grievous sickness, is so fine
So delicate and rare an ornament,
That it must lie in velvet and be set
Above the vulgar uses of the world.
I prayed for vengeance and the bitter draught
Bubbles before me, yet the icy grip
Of hatred slackens on my heart, and low
Thro' every silence comes the wailing cry
Of babes in pain.
                          Were it now well to leave
This old dead wrong in the unsleeping care
Of justice—to drop mercy on the need
Of even such a lying soul as looks
From yon beguiling eyes? The flushing lights
Of sunset fade, and a clear after-green

Steals o'er the west, as even draweth on.
In that last evening of our eager lives.
Their darker hopes must wither as a leaf
In furnace-fires, and love be all in all.

"Oh, Wilfred, Wilfred, this sad older Joan,
Would put the thoughts of vengeance from her soul
God knows, that now I look upon your face
Its weakness, passion, patience, I nor hate
Nor love you—but the child ? My wisest care
Shall wait in tenderness upon her needs.
You know not all the measure of that wrong
You wrought in our fair summer, God must lift
The darkness from your world-perverted soul,
In his good time. For me—I leave revenge
And hate and love behind, to work His will
In the dark ministry of pain. The child
Is His, not yours—mine even, if I stay
Her errant feet before they overstray
The brink of midnight's river——"

"Joan—forgive."

"I have forgiven. Richly as we love,
More richly yet, we women can forgive,
God-helping. Lead me hence. Yon after-light
Serene, and pale, and fading into night,
Is given, as presage of the fair regard,
Which from henceforth shall reign betwixt us two—
Until the end."

A WOMAN'S FAITH

WHILE the fourth Baldwin of Jerusalem
    Beneath the scourge
Of leprosy, yet lingered dark and deaf,
    But on the verge
Of that great freedom, which he nightly prayed—
    The Paynim host
Brake into fertile Galilee and smote
    From hill to coast,
Until the people pleaded with their king,
    For one to lead
The hasty levies forth against the foe.
    " In this our need
Oh Baldwin, let thy sister take Sir Guy,
    For wedded lord,
That as our future king, he may unsheathe
    Avenging sword."
So Sybille wedded Guy de Lusignan ;
    But had no love
To give the people's choice, for Raymond wore
    Her pearl-sewn glove,

And had she chosen, hand had gone with heart ;
    Yet having vowed
To be true wife, she willed to keep her oath,
    Until the shroud
Of sleep should still the patience-hidden pain.
    Sir Guy rode forth
To where the crafty Saracen lay camped
    Against the north—
As Christian knight, his reckless heart on fire,
    With one rare stroke,
To free the ravished land of Galilee
    From Paynim yoke.

Within his palace lay the dying king,
    The echoed clash
Of armour loud in his unhearing ears,
    And the hot flash
Of swords victorious striking thro' his dreams.
    There rose the cry
Of wondering citizens, and one awoke
    To prophesy
Of evil tidings, as a fugitive
    Way-worn, and red
With battle, clamoured at the city gate.
    As from the dead
Came Baldwin's answer to that unheard cry—
    " My God—I see
(For death has given more than sight) defeat
    They flee !   They flee !"

So died the king, and all the barons drew,
    But ill-content,
Around the Lady Sybille, muttering
    Of treasure spent—
A broken army—a foolhardy knight.
    But when she came
Thro' grey Jerusalem, white-robed, and fair
    As dawn, to claim
Her brother's crown, the common herd rejoiced,
    Shouting : "Sybille.
Queen of Jerusalem, by God's decree
    And our good will!"
Only in hall the nobles spake apart,
    Till from the dark
Full-armoured ranks stepped forth Heraclius
    The Patriarch,
With the brave counts of Thoron, Antioch,
    And Tripoli,
And many another—who in loyalty
    Had bent the knee
To Baldwin, but must measure fealty,
    When a weak hand
Was stretched towards the sceptre.   As a wave
    Breaks on the strand
And hushes, the hot shouting of the mob,
    Grew sharply still,
As the priest tempting while commanding, urged
    The council's will :—
"Sir Guy has failed in battle, is no man
    To stem the tide

Of ill-success, so is unmeet to wear
    The nation's bride—
Therefore we do declare the marriage void,
    De Lusignan
Once more a simple knight, and you maid-free
    To choose a man
As husband from this gathered chivalry—
    Raymond—Renaud—
Or any lesser knight.   And he on whom
    You shall bestow
Your love, shall be acknowledged as our king
    So swear we all!"
The sonorous reverberation rolled
    From wall to wall,
And those beyond the precincts of the court,
    With echoing shout
Returned a reverent "So swear we all."
    But in the doubt
Of that deep-voiced temptation, Sybille turned
    To where a cross
The emblem of renunciation hung ;
    And the near loss
Of one whose kingly arm had shielded life,
    As leaves a rose,
Rushed into memory.   Low kneeling there,
    By throne of those
Who knew not Godfrey's sad humility—
    She bent in prayer ;
For youth and love yet ruled her matron-pulse,
    And mother-care

Had never filled her day with its content.
　　But when she rose
It was as tho' some seraph-hand had brought
　　A deep repose
To all the yearnings of her woman's heart,—
　　So deep a calm
That Raymond felt his passion ebb, and stirred
　　In vague alarm,
Calling upon the saints. "I choose," she said,
　　And stepped between
The parting rank, with that slow step of kings,
　　Who seek with keen
And searching glance some trusty councillor.
　　So down the court
Of the great hall, she paced with lingering foot,
　　Till Raymond caught
Her passing glance, and fired it with his own ;
　　And suddenly,
A strange white anguish brake upon her brow,
　　And her bent knee
Trembled beneath her as she paused, the pain
　　· Of all she would
Resign, alive in her impassioned gaze.
　　A space she stood,
As one who asked forgiveness, and then turned
　　And down the hall
Past Geoffry, Jocelyn fared, till 'twixt her robe
　　And the grey wall,
Was only scorned De Lusignan. The queen
　　Looked on his face,

Until the depths of pity overflowed
    Till of her grace
She clasped her arms about him, and as wife
    Indignant cried,
"Sir Priest, whom God hath joined together, let
    Not man divide.
If I must choose again, my choice is here !
    So are you free,
To swear a wiser king—not braver knight—
    Your fealty.
The crown is but a circlet of red thorns,
    Which he may take
Who loves a painful hour."

              And as they heard,
    The people brake
Into a shout, but Sybille and her lord
    Went thro' the crowd,
All meekly on their way.

             So women cling
    When once is vowed
Their faith ; and this true legend of Sybille
    In every clime
Has touched the poet-hearts of troubadours
    To verse sublime.
A tale of sorrow, of a love which grew
    To bear the flower
Of stern renunciation—to lay all
    Of queenly power,

                    G

Of tender hope and dreaming, as a cloak
    That is out-worn
Behind—and so to pass clear-eyed—
    Nor all forlorn.
Strike ye the harp triumphantly, pour forth
    The glowing rhyme,
And send this tale of woman's faith adown
    The drifts of Time.

WHOM have I wronged? The dead, the quiet dead?
Nay, if I sinned it was against my God,
From whose far-seeing knowledge of the will
That yields to sudden and impatient throes
Of impulse, or is tainted from the birth—
Alone can fall a just impartial meed
Of chastening mercy. And altho' I loosed
The silver cord of life, it was with cold
Deliberate weighing of the present sin.
My sin—against a consequence of good—
That should enrich the after lives of those
Who were my nearest in this loneliness
Of social life—this bitter loneliness
Which like the wave about a swimmer holds
My spirit, tho' I strike it thro' and thro'
In eager search of—ah, I know not what—
A something kindred yet intangible
Which may be Love or Sympathy or God.
For me the haunting trouble of remorse
Is as the fear of babes, an ignorance
Of the unseen and powerful that runs
To easy dread. We dream of penalties
Beyond the sin, and oftent mes we stretch

The little, little fault into an ill
As vast as the dim vault above a world ;
But as for me—the dead is in its grave,
A hushed and half-forgotten lawlessness,
Of which my hand was guilty in the past—
And guilty before One who had engraved :
" This shalt thou do and this shalt thou avoid,"
Upon the living earnest of my soul.
Guilty—and therefore willing afterward
When I am cold in death, to strongly bear
Whatever penalty of consequence
Is fixed on the transgression.   Yet I live,
Walk, smile, and change a greeting with my kind ;
And that as calmly as the whitest soul
That ever set salvation above love;
While as for that long anguish of remorse
Which dull tradition would assign my days,
Making a subtle horror of the dark
And gnawing—gnawing till the heart of life
Quivers again beneath its poisoned fang—
What were its purpose—power—that it should dog
My footsteps thro' the pleasant ways of wealth ?
It could not give again the breath of life
To those still lips—nor would I have it given.
Nay, I would rather sin and sin again
Than hear her voice in other than my dreams—
Her living voice.   I counted all the cost
Before I mixed that drowsy draught of death ;
Counted it with a still regret that saw
The need—the consequence—

I do repent,
Acknowledge that my deed usurped the stern
Prerogative of Justice, yet rejoice
In that the deed is done.

＊　　　＊　　　＊　　　＊　　　＊　　　＊

A sunward clime
Lapped my unconscious infancy in scents,
And sights, and sounds, of oriental life ;
For I am child of one whose dusky eyes
Dwelt on an English soldier with the love
Of easterns, who forgot her home and race
For some few summers of idyllic love,
And died—contented.   I, their single hope
Was liker him in face, not fair, nor dark ;
A large-eyed babe, a silent dreamy child,
A woman in whose ears the rhythmic sounds
Of language, are for ever as a song
That all the world is singing.

Many years
Were lingered out beneath the peepul shade
Of the old garden, happy studious years
That added day to day, until I stood
Upon the golden edge of womanhood,
And heard my father's :

" Child, this flickering torch
Hath done its feeble work among the dark
And devious ways, and I may look again
Upon thy mother's face.   One of our kin—
The brother that is after me in years
And wealthy, hath the welcome of a love—

The love of early days, for me and mine;
And to his care, my tender one, I leave
Thy lands and thee." Thus, with a smile he passed,
And overseas upon the rugged shores
Of this grey isle, I found an honest heart
That in its broad excess of fatherhood
Could name me " child."

　　　　　　　　A stir of autumn wind
Was idly loosening the russet leaves,
As through the stoneway of an ancient gate
That for a many hundred years had frowned
Thro' lion-eyes upon the world, we turned.
And 'twixt the mighty spread of forest arms
I saw a vision as of dusky towers
Above a grey and ivied battlement ;
A mansion gloomy to my Indian eyes,
That missed the glow of marble and of gold ;
And yet with a grim beauty, as of piled
Rough rocks amid the softness of a glen.
On the white steps a deerhound stretched at ease
With long wise head upon the crossing paws,
And at his side, with trail of crimson leaves
Athwart her sombre robe, a lady stood
To listen, and the song upon her lips
Ceased in a smile, as from beneath the gloom
Of stretching boughs, we drove into the warm
Late flushes of the light.

　　　　　　　" Doris, I bring
A sister to your care," and the deep eyes

Grey as the shifting shadows of the gloam,
Lifted a wistful question : " Father mine,
She cannot know that all these eighteen years
I have been listening for a sister's voice,
Which is not the less welcome that it comes
So late—so late."

Thus were we lightly launched
Upon the calm and heaven-azured mere
Of sister-love ; tho' as the peaceful years
Went bravely forward at the call of Time,
Our pleasure-vessels turned and floated down
Towards the deep, the deep that was to set
A tide of stronger love between our lives,
In chill division.

Every kindling fire
Hath a young glow of flame from which it spreads,
Until it grasp a rotten bough—a tree—
And all the forest burns.   So the events—
The wide unquiet changings of my day,
Run finely back into a point of time,
Remembered—oh, my heart, so well—so well !
The heir of a bucolic house had come
To man's estate, and all the county-world
Must gather in his father's hall.   We danced
In a long chamber hung with fairy green,
On high the crimson of a flaunting flag,
And mosses with a trail of ivy hung
About the rounded mirrors.   From the low

Age-blackened rafters swung the golden lamps,
Shedding the softness of a tinted gleam
Upon the shifting pageant, that was set
Now in the glamour of a dance, anon
Changed as a rainbow into points of light
Beneath the palms, or in the twilight-depths
Of a dim-shadowed bower. And Doris stood
In green of spring, with, as it were, a growth
Of nodding chiming lilies at her feet,
Sweet lily-bells that fill the woodland vales
With fragrance, and must nestle at her throat,
Nestle and sleep in the soft billowy dusk
Of coiled and gathered tresses, nestle deep
In every verdurous light silken fold,
Until we called her " lilied maid," as sweet
As any nodding lily, and as fair.
But I was paler in a pansy-gown,
With glow of eastern gold in tracery
Of mystic forms upon the purple edge
Of sleeve and skirt. And o'er the polished oak
Of the long floor, we glided in the dance,
Until the dawn was loosening a flight
Of keen and frosty shafts upon the world.
From sundown until break of day our feet
Went tirelessly, and either danced again
And yet again with Kenneth Leigh, a man
Stalwart, erect, and yet as roughly hewn
As any clansman of moss-trooping days.
And as we talked thro' the mid-winter morn,
With all our bravery of silken gowns

Thrown lightly by it was of Kenneth Leigh.
" He came but yesterday from France and stays
The sennight here," I whispered, with a strange
New envy rankling bitter in my thought.
Alas, that Doris should look greyly out
Of such clear eyes, should walk so maiden fair,
When the hot flushes of my heart were warm,
Oh warm again as any western thought ;
And the dim possibility of life,
Intenser, passionate, already seen
As far bright lakes beyond the desert sand ;
And yet, and yet, if love should hesitate
Betwixt our hearts, I could have yielded it—
Ay, even then, for Doris was more dear
Than self.

       The glowing whiteness of the dawn,
A chill ecstatic light which slowly parts
And brightens into day, drew freshly on
Towards the noon, and day succeeded day
Until the week had numbered all its hours.
And evermore my yearning thought must wait
On Kenneth standing in the window depths
With Doris, on the careful strength that taught
Her feet to strike across the frozen mere,
The ear that heard her voice among the crowd,
So soft and sweet a voice, the listener
Must bend to hearken. Yet an afterthought
Was ever lurking sombre by the stern
And overhanging level of his brows ;
An afterthought that was not all of peace,

Although the shyness of a happiness
Too deep for words, was shining under dusk
Of downward lashes and for him alone.

The sennight passed, and Kenneth stretched a hand
In farewell to the circle—last to her.
And I, whose heart was tossing on a sea
Of bitter, bitter pain, must watch the clasp,
Until I read their faces like a scroll
On temple wall.   An anguish as of death,
Or of a soul in torment, answered back
The wistful questioning that Doris raised,
A questioning that had forgot the world,
And self, and all—that only craved to share
The reason of his pain—the pain itself.
We were in little groups about the hall,
And as the sound of wheels upon the road,
Died in a rolling echo, the old squire
Must shake his hoary head : " A likely lad,
Too good for such as Agnes Huntingdon,
Although he chanced to override her beast
That morning in the field."   And in the dim
Uncertain gloam through which the sudden leap
And flicker of the flames broke redly bright,
A burning tear-drop fell.   Some cruel chance
Had kept the story of a careless ride
And its misplaced remorse, from either ear,
And one had walked towards the gate of heaven,
Only to find the darkness of a pit

Before the widening doors.   No fault of his,
Who thought the story known, and yet a fault
In that he lingered at her side, and won
So true a heart again.   For Doris spake
In all the after moments of our life,
No more of love, but lived her quiet days
In the exceeding patience of a soul,
That waits and waits, until the flight of time
Shall bring a newer hope, a fairer day.
While I, whose dull unhappy restlessness,
An ache, a covered hurt, would send me forth
As sea-bird on the arid waste of life,
Had but a memory of conventional
Dull words, of days that held nor love, nor hope,
But the one presence of the soul beloved ;
Days when the sun had shone, though not on me,
Who was a forest flower so deeply set
In mosses, and the shade of leafy boughs,
That never ray of heaven's light might fall
Across its blanching leaves.

                                       The billowy tide
Had turned and drifted through opposing bars,
To set a width of sad and murmuring sea
Betwixt our sister lives ; and I was fain
To wander till the hurt was overlaid
By drift of trifles, such as time will leave
In deepest crevasse of a seaward rock ;
Ay, and until I wearied of the change
Incessant, various; of the shifting scenes—

The clamour, clatter, of a foreign tongue—
And turned with a sick longing in my heart,
To verdurous deep glooms, the solitude
Of many waters, and the storied halls
Wherein my father wakened to the light.

A belt of gloomy woods—so needle-dark
That in their shade the bramble bloomed alone
And never rabbit burrowed—girt the house,
An old red pile, with unexpected stairs
And passages into a secret room,
Where legendary kings had lain concealed
In other days ; a quaint and curious place,
With stains of blood in the long gallery,
To hint a story of the murderous dead—
Their loves, their passions, and their nothingness ;
As after men will point at what I build,
Saying, "A silent woman, who nor loved
Nor hated, but has lived her little life,
And left the record of these added bricks
To say she breathed."

                              A crumbling line of wall,
Beneath whose grey and ancient coping-stone
The curling hartstongue showed a narrow leaf,
And delicate wild grasses found a depth
Of moist dark earth wherein to root and grow—
A wall with many a gap and fallen stone,
But yet a wall which marked the boundary
Betwixt my meadows and the barren land
Which yet remained to Kenneth of the broad

And golden acres which his mother gave -
A wall which ran beside me as I walked.
Till one, with elbows on the mossy edge,
Laughed me a greeting.   Through the tender green
Of the young larches I could see a face,
Mischievous, bold—the face of Agnes Leigh !
The face of one I hated, yet for whom
I found an answering smile, the neighbour-clasp
Of slim dark hands, and a light confidence---
The trifles of a day.   For Agnes Leigh
Had kindled the slow passion of despair
In a deep heart that hid the rising flame,
And let it eat and eat into his life ;
Her ways unwifely were the county talk,
Her scattering of gold, her brazen words
And reckless gallops, gave the nodding heads
A wherewithal to prophesy the end ;
Yet for the sake of a sweet memory,
A sometime love, I smiled into her eyes,
And was her friend—if service be the test
Of all beyond a casual touch of hands.
We rode together through the leafy ways,
And marked the kestrel wheeling in the blue,
The stir of white as a brown rabbit coursed
Across the open, and the flirting wings
Of a long-widowed pie ; and as we stretched
Across the uplands with the honey-gorse
Around, beyond, a sea of deepening light,
I took—and with a smile—the cooler bows
Of those who thought to cavil at my friend.

It was for Kenneth's sake—Kenneth, who groaned
Beneath a load of debt, and lashed his foes
With whip of bitter and satiric words,
When moved beyond endurance ; Kenneth Leigh,
Alas, a man that had been sweet of soul
And kindly as a laughing three-year babe,
Before the acid of a long regret
Had curdled all his thought.   A friendly gleam
Ran through his smile, when on a lonely walk
Our ways encountered ; yet the smile was *hers*,
And I, her friend—no more.   Oh ! Doris Rhys,
I have indeed been friend to thee and thine,
And loyal, though a fierce temptation beat
And clamoured in the courtyard of my soul.
Ay, loyal ever—though the tale I told,
The tale of thy unwedded patient faith,
Was as the passing of my latest hope.

On a fresh morrow of the budding May,
When promise of the coming fruit was white
O'er all the land, and every ferny frond
Was slow uncurling in the hedge, we sat,
Agnes and I, beside a spark of fire
In the deserted hall, and, with a glance
Into my quiet face, as one who asked
The thought beneath, she drew a written page
From the loose purple foldings of her gown.
"The farce is played, Yasora."   And she shred
The budding lilac from its numerous
Small stems, as one who, inly resolute,

Yet trembles at the darkness and the depth
Of the dim gulf, whereto her feet have strayed.
Gloom suddenly upon her steadfast gaze.
" The farce is fully played, and now I read
The prologue of a drama.   Long ago,
You sought to build the barrier of space
Betwixt my love—my soldier love—and me.
You sent him forth with a last honest word
Of farewell on his lips, and would have kept
My straying feet in the domestic path.
Alas the fates are stronger than your will,
And now—you tremble, but the risk is mine,
The risk, the joy, the heaven !   He cannot live
Without me, and I—I have never loved
Other than Kenneth's gold—the glittering heaps
That I have scattered, as an autumn breeze
Scatters the fallen leafage of the woods.
Why should I linger when a proven love
Is waiting?   Hush ! your words are as the fall
Of raindrops on a scarred and rocky ground,
And I am deaf to what you urge.   Of all
The millions under heaven, you alone
Have been my friend, but neither you nor they
Can stay me now.   'My husband?' he will learn
In a sharp school, that calm perfunctory love
Is not enough to keep a woman true.
He has been kind, forbearing—oh I grant
His virtues, but this other is my love.
' The children?' I am no poetic soul,
To find a beauty in the natural ways

And wants of children, rather I would keep
A staff of nurses to relieve my hands
Of every mother-duty."   And she laughed
Until an echo caught the cruel tones ;
And merriment of multiplying fiends
Broke from the further wall.   I heard—and lo,
A memory of sinister refrain
Cried from the midnight bosom of the past,
As once again the blue of India's sea
Sparkled between the sudden dark of boughs ;
And glistening sails, as separated pearls
Gleamed, in their course, above the sapphire depths,
While the soft accents of an eastern tongue
Sank thro' my listening, as the creeping tides
Thro' the sun-hardened surface of the sand.

" This phial daughter was prepared of those
Who dwell among the hills ; a skilful race,
That in the silence of the moony night
Distil a herbal poison, one that leaves
No trace betraying, and whereof a draught
Of six clear drops, six pale and tasteless drops,
Can lessen the heart's action unto sleep—
A sleep my child that has no after-thought
Of dreams or wakening.   It came to me
From one who owed thy mother, neither life
Nor hope nor liberty, but only love—
And shall be thine.   Some hour of utmost need
May render death a sour-sweet remedy,
May bid us choose between a tainted joy

And the long silence—death and sin !   Oh, take
The lesser ill."

        A delicate fine cup
Glittered before me in the ruddy light
Of rousing flames, and the small phial lay
Above my heart.   She called her husband "good
And hoped to cast a stain upon his name,
A clinging stain that neither time nor change
Might wholly cleanse from memory of man.
Death or dishonour ? ay, the lesser ill
Were death.   I drew the flask into my hand
Nor felt it tremble, praised the glowing skies
Until she rose to look upon the piled
Red glory of the clouds, nor ever heard
A strangeness in my voice.   "The western heavens
Are battle-stained, and gorgeous with the glint
Of golden harness.   From the further clouds
Leaps the red levin-flash."   And six clear drops
Sank thro' the coffee as she gazed :—

                "Oh ay !
A pretty glow of yellow, red and blue,
But crude, barbaric.   Rake the resinous
Brown cones together in a cheery blaze,
And draw a-nigh that I may see your face ;
I think its dark and earnest smile will haunt
My last long dreams, as tho' it overlaid
A mystery, the which I cannot probe,
But which concerns me.   How the cruel flames

                                H

Leap up, and laugh, and crackle round the wood,
Throwing their shadows in a devil's dance
Uncouth and weird upon the further wall !
This coffee "—and she drank as one athirst—
" This coffee hath the genuine Mocha taste,
And is as fragrant as the golden wines
Of old Tokay.   Yasora in the past,
The past that you have buried fathoms deep,
Did ever glance of lover stir your heart,
And waken passion till the placid stream
Of life, was quickened to a rush of fire ?
Or did he plead, and plead to be refused,
And so—unhappy—pass.   You were not loved ?
Then am I richer far, who held the love
Of Kenneth from the first, and hold it now,
Ay, and of others.   I am wondrous dull !
Not altogether tired, but near to sleep,
And languid—fold the skins about my feet,
And let me sink into a happy dream—
A long, long dream of love——"

                       And Agnes slept—
The weary limbs relaxing as her lids
Shut out the shadows of the creeping night—
Her night, that not an arrow of the dawn
Might shatter—a long night of dreams—perchance
Of rest so deep that even dreams are dulled
Into forgetfulness.   I watched the slow
Deep heavings of her breast, until they came
More slowly yet and ceased.   Repentance ?   Fear ?

They run not in my blood.   The deed was done,
Done for all time and any pale remorse
Had seemed the veriest impotence of fear.

As with a lion-skin about her feet
She lay unbreathing, warm—I found her fair ;
Fair, tho' the touch of every reckless hour
Had left a deepened line about her lips—
A child's lips once, lips that in death were drawn
Into a smile, the smile of one who dreams
An innocent glad dream.   I laid my lips
A-quiver with regretful tenderness,
On the broad brow.   I had not loved her well,
And now the mystery of death—my gift—
Was softening her follies, and her sins,
Into a memory not wholly ill.
A letter lay between the folded hands—
His letter—and I laid it on the cones,
Watching it curl and blacken till a grey
Of fluttered ash was dancing in the flames,
And only a wan woman lay and dreamed
Her "long, long dream of love."   Ay, long indeed,
So long, the greatest length of earthly days
Were but as the quick moments of its youth.

"A failure of heart's action," said the wise,
Wording a learned scientific why ;
 Above the silent couch ; and if I smiled,
It was in scorn of what a western world
Esteems as very learned.   Agnes lay

With some six drops of sleep about her heart,
And any savage woman of the hills
Had smiled a wiser reading of her sleep
Into mine eyes. "A failure of the heart?"
Oh ay—the loosing of the silver cord,
The shatt'ring of a bowl, not gold, nor good,
But very earthen—any set of words
That will convey the master-note of death.
Death—the unsmiling mystery that bears
Our shrinking bodies from the shores of day,
And love, and knowledge, as the hungry sea
Will creep about a boat that has been left
In sandy creek, and float it from the land.
Death—about whom the creeds of every land
Must dogmatise—death and the future hope,
The hope of love's re-union, of a life
More beautiful and nearer the divine.
A hope? Ay, that alone, tho' every sect
Clamour "Behold the truth," and would accept
The dreamy guessings of its holy men
As knowledge—for the consciousness Divine
Is throned in silence. Man has dared to weave
His human fables round the primal fact
Of God and love, yet—when the woven strands
Have rotted back into their elements,
Love will emerge the heart of every creed,
Its knowledge and its truth. To serve and trust
To serve in life and trust upon the brink
Of what may be a silence or a birth—
A doom or a decay. We cannot know

But one more loving, than the saddest soul,
That wanders lonely over earth can hope—
Retains the secret of our destiny,
And bids us trust.

      I followed when the tramp
Of measured feet would bear a coffin thence,
And all the world was moving soberly.
For tho' we shatter monarchy and cry
" There is no God," the boldest bows a knee
When the death-pageant glooms upon his view.
The bursting blossom of the May, in bud
And bloom and scented lily, lay enwreathed
Above the stirless smile of Agnes Leigh—
The smile that I had lighted.   Trill of birds
Brake from the ivy of a Norman arch,
As the slow service overtold her hopes
Of the hereafter ; and the deepening day
That erst had flung a gust of windy rain
Across the weald, now swept her veil aside
And smiled in sudden sunshine of the spring ;
While in my heart the smile of Agnes Leigh
Was ever shining brighter than the day,
Ay, and shall shine in grey or gloom or gold,
Until I too am laid as " earth to earth."

  *   *   *   *   *

The pines have tossed their branches thro' a week
Of stormy winters, since I ventured all—
My all on that May eve ; and now as wife,
A worthier wife than she who sleeps and sleeps

Beneath the sombre sighing of the yews,
My Doris reigns in the old Manor-House.
I am beyond the gates, a soul that yearned
For other than the husks of human love—
A soul that never may be satisfied,
And so is half-content to sit and watch
The deepening of a happy matron-smile
In eyes beloved.   The children hold me dear,
Treading a little pathway thro' the woods
That stretch between our homes ; and Kenneth's laugh
Falls on my heart as a sweet sometime song,
For which we listen thro' the noon and hear
As the night-shadows fall across the corn—
Content so we have heard it ere we sleep.
I sinned, and the reward is happiness,
The happiness of those whom I have loved
Beyond my God—myself.   A white reward,
That should forget the chill of loneliness
For ever pressing—pressing on my heart.

Yet as I dream, a dark suggestion falls
Out of the woven fancies.   It may be
That a diviner purpose than the peace
Of wedded love hath underlain our lives ;
That from the fire of love's imperious pain,
Our souls had hoped to issue free of earth
As any ore that passes thro' the flame.
And if this be—if life be such a dream,
Given in mystery and laboured thro'
Until we pierce that later mystery

Which will enfold us from the light of day
Then have I sinned indeed, who thought to mend
The natural order, with presumptuous hand
Making and marring. But our human "ifs"
Are never lifted into certainty,
And if my sin was greater than I dream—
Lo! I am more than ready to endure
Its after consequence of pain, to toil
And suffer till my spirit is absolved
Of guilt, and I am even as a child,
A little child that sins and is forgiven.
I could not clamour at the gates of heaven
For a mere pardon, till my eager soul
Had proved its penitence, had wrought and grieved
And gathered the dim wage of death.   We sin—
We suffer ; for the sometime punishment
Of evil deeds, is sure as ebb and flow
Of the moon-tides, but our forgiveness lies
In the deep heart of love.   If we are born
To urgings of inherited desire
Which bear us into crime, and sin, and shame,
The God, who giving life, foresaw its will,
Faulty, uncertain, full of whims and hopes,
Impulses, turmoils, passions, can decide
On what is due to nature, heritage,
Surrounding circumstance, or actual sin.
Our human breath—the gift of God—unasked
Yet treasured—has been poured into dim souls,
All flawed and flecked, the children of a race
Imperfect, evil ; but the Lord of Life

Yielding us breath, can view our shifts and shames
As mothers view the stumblings of a child,
Crippled at birth.   So be it with my sin.
Perchance this hurt which knows no earthly balm
Is punishment enough for such a soul.
To love and long—ah me !   To know that time
Can never bring relief!   To love, and find
A constancy that never wintry frosts
May hope to wither, a white hopeless faith,
That stands a blasted stem among the green
And fruiting monarchs of the orchard depths.

The children cling about me, with rough arms
Clasping me round and crushing all my film
Of laces, as they crushed the daisy-buds
Beneath their hasty feet.   Oh sweet rough arms
And loving hasty feet, I could not spare
One kiss for all the laces in the world,
One rushing step for all the daisy-buds
That ever the spring showered into life.
Your mother? but alas the memory
Which should be holiest to childhood stirs
Nor tear nor wistful cry.   I did not sin
Oh baby-hearts so deeply, hold me close,
And kiss away this hurt that stirs my soul
To a perpetual unrest.

Printed by BALLANTYNE, HANSON & CO.
London and Edinburgh

A Selection

FROM

MR. WM. HEINEMANN'S LIST

March 1892.

The Crown Copyright Series.

Mr. Heinemann has made arrangements with a number of the first and most popular authors. English,

ENGLISH, AMERICAN, AND COLONIAL,

which will enable him to issue a Series of new and original works to be known as the CROWN COPY-RIGHT SERIES at a uniform price of FIVE SHILLINGS per volume.

These novels will not pass through an expensive two or three volume edition, but they will be obtainable at the Circulating Libraries as well as at all Booksellers and Bookstalls.

The following volumes are now ready:—

ACCORDING TO ST. JOHN. By Amélie Rives, Author of "The Quick or the Dead," &c.

THE PENANCE OF PORTIA JAMES. By "Tasma," Author of "Uncle Piper of Piper's Hill," &c.

INCONSEQUENT LIVES. A Village Chronicle, Shewing how certain Folk set out for El Dorado, What they Attempted, and What they Attained. By J. H. Pearce, Author of "Esther Pentreath," &c.

In the Press.

A QUESTION OF TASTE. By Maarten Maartens, Author of "The Sin of Joost Avelingh," &c.

COME LIVE WITH ME AND BE MY LOVE. By Robert Buchanan.

THE O'CONNORS OF BALLINAHINCH. By Mrs. Hungerford, Author of "Molly Bawn."

A BATTLE AND A BOY. By Blanche Willis Howard, Author of "Guenn," &c.

Heinemann's International Library.

Edited by EDMUND GOSSE. Price 3s. 6d. cloth, 2s. 6d. paper.

New Review.—"If you have any pernicious remnants of literary chauvinism, I hope it will not survive the series of foreign classics of which Mr. William Heinemann, aided by Mr. Edmund Gosse, is publishing translations to the great contentment of all lovers of literature."

Times.—"A venture which deserves encouragement."

** Each Volume has an Introduction specially written by the Editor.

IN GOD'S WAY. From the Norwegian of BJÖRNSTJERNE BJÖRNSON.

Athenæum.—"There are descriptions which certainly belong to the best and cleverest things our literature has ever produced."

PIERRE AND JEAN. From the French of GUY DE MAUPASSANT.

Pall Mall Gazette.—"It is admirable from beginning to end."

THE CHIEF JUSTICE. From the German of KARL EMIL FRANZOS, Author of "For the Right," &c.

New Review.—"Few novels of recent times have a more sustained and vivid human interest."

WORK WHILE YE HAVE THE LIGHT. From the Russian of COUNT TOLSTOY.

Scotsman.—"It is impossible to convey any adequate idea of the simplicity and force with which the work is unfolded."

FANTASY. From the Italian of MATILDE SERAO.

Scottish Leader.—"It is a work of elfish art, a mosaic of life and love, of right and wrong, of human weakness and strength, and purity and wantonness pieced together in deft and witching precision."

FROTH. From the Spanish of DON ARMANDO PALACIO VALDÉS.

Daily Telegraph.—"Vigorous and powerful in the highest degree. . . . . Rare and graphic strength."

FOOTSTEPS OF FATE. From the Dutch of LOUIS COUPERUS.

PEPITA JIMÉNEZ. From the Spanish of JUAN VALERA.

THE COMMODORE'S DAUGHTERS. From the Norwegian of JONAS LIE.

FLAGS ARE FLYING. From the Norwegian of BJÖRNSTJERNE BJÖRNSON.

Heinemann's 3s. 6d. Novels.

UNCLE PIPER OF PIPER'S HILL. By "TASMA," Author of "The Penance of Portia James," &c.

A MARKED MAN. Some Episodes in his Life. By ADA CAMBRIDGE.

Pall Mall.—"Contains one of the best written stories of a *mésalliance* that is to be found in modern fiction."

IN THE VALLEY. By HAROLD FREDERIC. Illustrated.

Athenæum.—"A novel deserving to be read."

THE THREE MISS KINGS. By ADA CAMBRIDGE.

British Weekly.—"A novel to be bought and kept for re-reading on languid summer afternoons or stormy winter evenings.

PRETTY MISS SMITH. By FLORENCE WARDEN.

Punch.—"Since the 'House on the Marsh,' I have not read a more exciting tale."

A ROMANCE OF THE CAPE FRONTIER. By BERTRAM MITFORD.

Observer.—" A rattling tale—genial, healthy, and spirited."

THE BONDMAN. By HALL CAINE.

Academy.—"A splendid novel."

A MODERN MARRIAGE. By the MARQUISE CLARA LANZA.

Queen.—"A powerful story."

LOS CERRITOS. A Romance of the Modern Time. By GERTRUDE FRANKLIN ATHERTON.

Athenæum.—"A decidedly charming romance."

DAUGHTERS OF MEN. By HANNAH LYNCH. Author of "The Prince of the Glades," &c. [*Shortly.*

New Works of Fiction.

NOR WIFE, NOR MAID. By Mrs. HUNGER-
FORD, Author of "Molly Bawn," &c. In Three Vols.

NOT ALL IN VAIN. By ADA CAMBRIDGE,
Author of "A Marked Man," &c. In Three Vols.

THE SCAPEGOAT. By HALL CAINE, Author
of "The Bondman." Fourth Edition. In Two Vols.

MAMMON. By Mrs. ALEXANDER, Author of
"The Wooing O't," &c. In Three Vols.

THE MOMENT AFTER. A Tale of the
Unseen. By ROBERT BUCHANAN. Popular Edition,
crown 8vo, 1s.

In Preparation.

**THE NAULAKHA: A Tale of West and
East.** By RUDYARD KIPLING and WOLCOTT BALESTIER.
In One Volume, crown 8vo.

THE AVERAGE WOMAN. Containing, A
Common Story, Reffey, and Captain My Captain. By
WOLCOTT BALESTIER. With a Portrait of the Author, and
an Introduction by Henry James. In One Vol., crown 8vo.

WOMAN AND THE MAN. By ROBERT
BUCHANAN. In Two Vols.

LITTLE JOHANNES. A Fairy Tale. By
F. VAN EEDEN. Translated from the Dutch, by CLARA
BELL, with an Introduction by ANDREW LANG, and Illus-
trations. In One Volume.

THE TOWER OF TADDEO. By OUIDA,
Author of "Two Little Wooden Shoes," &c.

ORIOLE'S DAUGHTER. By JESSIE FOTHER-
GILL, Author of "The First Violin," &c. In Three Vols.

THE WHITE FEATHER. By "TASMA." In
Three Vols.

THE HEAD OF THE FIRM. By Mrs.
RIDDELL, Author of "George Geith," &c. In Three Vols.

VANITAS. By VERNON LEE, Author of "Haunt-
ings," &c.

The Drama.

THE DRAMATIC WORKS OF ARTHUR
W. PINERO. Published in Monthly Volumes, each containing a Complete Play, with its Stage History. Price 1s. 6d. paper cover, 2s. 6d. cloth extra.

VOL. I. The Times.

II. The Profligate.
With a Portrait.

III. The Cabinet
Minister.

VOL. IV. The Hobby-
Horse.

VOL. V. Lady Bountiful.
In April.

₊ To be followed by the Author's other Plays.

NERO AND ACTEA. A Tragedy. By ERIC
MACKAY, Author of "A Lover's Litanies," and "Love Letters of a Violinist." Crown 8vo, 5s.

HEDDA GABLER. A Drama in Four Acts.
By HENRIK IBSEN. Translated from the Norwegian by EDMUND GOSSE. Library edition, with Portrait, small 4to, 5s. Vaudeville Edition, paper, 1s.

₊ Also a limited large paper edition, with three portraits, 21s. net.

THE FRUITS OF ENLIGHTENMENT.
A Comedy in Four Acts. By LYOF TOLSTOY. Translated from the Russian by E. J. DILLON. With an Introduction by A. W. PINERO, and a Portrait of the Author. Small 4to, 5s.

THE PRINCESS MALEINE. Translated
from the French by GERARD HARRY; and THE IN-
TRUDER. By MAURICE MAETERLINCK. Translated from the French. With an Introduction by HALL CAINE. Small 4to, with a Portrait. 5s.

STRAY MEMORIES. By ELLEN TERRY.
One Volume, Illustrated. *[In the Press.*

THE LIFE OF HENRIK IBSEN. By
HENRIK JÆGER. Translated by CLARA BELL. With the Verse done into English from the Norwegian original by EDMUND GOSSE. In One Volume, crown 8vo, 6s.

SOME INTERESTING FALLACIES OF
THE MODERN STAGE. An Address delivered to the Playgoers' Club at St. James's Hall, on Sunday, 6th December, 1891. By HERBERT BEERHOHM TREE. Crown 8vo, sewed, 6d.

Miscellaneous.

THE JEW AT HOME. By JOSEPH PENNELL. With Illustrations by the Author. 4to.   [*In the Press.*

IDYLLS OF WOMANHOOD. Poems. By AMY DAWSON. Foolscap 8vo, gilt top, 5s.

THE LITTLE MANX NATION. By HALL CAINE, Author of "The Bondman." Crown 8vo, cloth, 3s. 6d.; paper, 2s. 6d.

GIRLS AND WOMEN. By E. CHESTER. Pott 8vo, 2s. 6d., or gilt extra, 3s. 6d.

GOSSIP IN A LIBRARY. By EDMUND GOSSE. Second Edition. Crown 8vo, gilt top, 7s. 6d.

₊ Large Paper Edition, limited to 100 copies. Price on application.

THE CANADIAN GUIDE-BOOK. The Tourist's and Sportsman's Guide to Eastern Canada and Newfoundland, including all descriptions of Routes, Cities, Points of Interest, Summer Resorts, Fishing Places, &c. With an Appendix giving fish and game laws, and Official Lists of Trout and Salmon Rivers and their Lessees. By CHARLES G. D. ROBERTS. With Maps and many Illustrations. Crown 8vo, limp cloth.

WOMAN—THROUGH A MAN'S EYE-GLASS. By MALCOLM C. SALAMAN. With Illustrations by DUDLEY HARDY.   [*In the Press.*

THE WORKS OF HEINRICH HEINE. Translated by CHARLES G. LELAND, F.R.L.S., M.A. Volume I.—Florentine Nights, Schnabelewopski. The Rabbi of Bacharach, and Shakespeare's Maidens and Women. Volumes II. and III., Pictures of Travel. In Two Volumes. Volume IV., The Book of Songs. Volumes V. and VI., Germany. In Two Volumes. Crown 8vo, 5s. each.

DE QUINCEY MEMORIALS. Edited by
ALEXANDER H. JAPP, LL.D., F.R.S.E. In Two Volumes,
demy 8vo, with portrait, 30s. net.

THE POSTHUMOUS WORKS OF
THOMAS DE QUINCEY. Edited by ALEXANDER H.
JAPP, LL.D., F.R.S.E. Volume I. Suspiria de Profundis
and other Essays. Crown 8vo, 6s.

THE GENTLE ART OF MAKING ENE-
MIES. By J. M'NEILL WHISTLER. In One Volume,
pott 4to, 10s. 6d. Also, 150 Copies on Hand-made Paper,
Numbered and Signed by the Author, £2 2s. each.

THE COMING TERROR, and other Essays
and Letters. By ROBERT BUCHANAN. Second Edition.
Demy 8vo, 12s. 6d.

IMPERIAL GERMANY. A Critical Study of
Fact and Character. By SIDNEY WHITMAN. Crown 8vo,
cloth, 2s. 6d.; paper 2s.

DENMARK: Its History, Topography, Language,
Literature, Fine Arts, Social Life, and Finance. Edited
by H. WEITMEYER. With Coloured Map. In One
Volume, 8vo, 12s. 6d. Dedicated by permission to H.R.H.
the Princess of Wales.

THE GENESIS OF THE UNITED
STATES. A Narrative of the Movement in England 1605-
1616, which resulted in the Plantation of North America by
Englishmen. By ALEXANDER BROWN, F.R.H.S., &c. &c.
In Two Volumes, 8vo, with numerous maps, plans, portraits,
autographs, &c., £3 13s. 6d.

THE GARDEN'S STORY; or, Pleasures and
Trials of an Amateur Gardener. By G. H. ELLWANGER.
With an Introduction by the Rev. C. WOLLEY DOD.
One Volume, fcap. 8vo, illustrated, 5s.

THE WORD OF THE LORD UPON THE

WATERS. Sermons read by His Imperial Majesty the Emperor of Germany while at Sea, on his Voyages to the Land of the Midnight Sun. Composed by Dr. RICHTER, Army Chaplain, and Translated from the German by JOHN R. MCILRAITH. 4to, cloth, 2s. 6d.

THE PASSION PLAY AT OBERAM-

MERGAU, 1890. By F. W. FARRAR, D.D., F.R.S., Archdeacon and Canon of Westminster. In One Volume, 4to, cloth, 2s. 6d.

THE LABOUR MOVEMENT IN

AMERICA. By RICHARD T. ELY, Ph.D., Associate in Political Economy, Johns Hopkins University. In One Volume, crown 8vo, 5s.

Heinemann's Scientific Handbooks.

GEODESY. By J. HOWARD GORE. Small crown 8vo, illustrated, cloth, 5s.

MANUAL OF ASSAYING GOLD, SILVER,

COPPER, and LEAD ORES. By WALTER LEE BROWN, B.Sc. With a Chapter on the ASSAYING OF FUEL, by A. B. GRIFFITHS, Ph.D., F.R.S., F.C.S. Small crown 8vo, illustrated, cloth, 7s. 6d.

Colliery Guardian.—" A delightful and fascinating book."

THE PHYSICAL PROPERTIES OF

GASES. By ARTHUR L. KIMBALL. Small crown 8vo, illustrated, cloth, 5s.

Chemical News.—"The man of culture who wishes for a general and accurate acquaintance with the physical properties of gases will find in Mr. Kimball's work just what he requires."

HEAT AS A FORM OF ENERGY. By

Professor R. H. THURSTON. Small crown 8vo, illustrated, cloth, 5s.

Chemical News.—This work will prove both welcome and useful."

www.ingramcontent.com/pod-product-compliance
Lightning Source LLC
Chambersburg PA
CBHW032007010726
47493CB00007B/2301